"No."

This was beginning to sound much more favorable. "And we wouldn't be sleeping together?"

The corner of Alex's lip curved up, yet his eyes darkened. "This isn't make-believe, Olivia. It would be a real marriage."

Her stomach flipped at the thought of them in bed together.

Making love.

"I swore I'd never marry again."

His eyes took on a softer look. "This wouldn't be for love, Olivia. You wouldn't have to worry about me hurting you."

She wasn't so sure about that.

Dear Reader,

I must admit that when I read about those high-profile couples who marry, I sometimes wonder if it's for love or convenience. And if it's for convenience, what goes on behind the scenes? Why do you marry someone you don't know or don't love? *How* do you? You'd surely have to feel some sort of attraction for the other person to make it a real marriage.

This is the case between Olivia Cannington and Alex Valente, the heroine and hero in my book. Born with silver spoons in their mouths, they have the responsibility of having to marry for a year for reasons other than themselves. Neither has any intention of getting emotionally involved, but in the end it's their attraction for each other that sabotages them, and they eventually find their sacrifice hasn't been the sacrifice they thought it was. They fall in love.

Sometimes it takes a while for some people to realize it, but whether rich or poor, if you have true love you have it all.

Happy reading!

Maxine

MAXINE SULLIVAN

THE CEO TAKES A WIFE

Silhouette®

Desire

Published by Silhouette Books

America's Publisher of Contemporary Romance

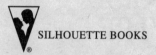

SILHOUETTE BOOKS

ISBN-13: 978-0-373-76883-7
ISBN-10:   0-373-76883-4

THE CEO TAKES A WIFE

Copyright © 2008 by Maxine Sullivan

Books by Maxine Sullivan

Silhouette Desire

The Millionaire's Seductive Revenge #1782
The Tycoon's Blackmailed Mistress #1800
The Executive's Vengeful Seduction #1818
Mistress & a Million Dollars #1855
The CEO Takes a Wife #1883

*Australian Millionaires

MAXINE SULLIVAN

credits her mother for her lifelong love of romance novels, so it was a natural extension for Maxine to want to write her own romances. She thinks there's nothing better than being a writer and is thrilled to be one of the few Australians to write for the Silhouette Desire line.

Maxine lives in Melbourne, Australia, but over the years has traveled to New Zealand, the UK and the USA. In her own backyard, her husband's job ensured they saw the diversity of the countryside, from the tropics to the outback, country towns to the cities. She is married to Geoff, who has proven his hero status many times over the years. They have two handsome sons and an assortment of much-loved, previously abandoned animals.

Maxine would love to hear from you and can be contacted through her Web site at http://www.maxinesullivan.com.

To all my workmates at my day job.
Thanks for all your support and enthusiasm.

One

"I presume you asked me in here for a reason, Dad?" Alex Valente said, his tone cool and collected as he sat in front of his father's desk in the opulent tenth-floor office overlooking Sydney Harbour.

There was a moment's pause. "Yes, there's a reason," Cesare Valente replied, leaning back in his leather chair.

Alex ignored the mixture of pride and regret in his father's eyes. They'd never been close, despite working together all these years. Cesare Valente had come to Australia as a child and was the founder of the House of Valente. Alex was its CEO. The two of them had taken the Australian perfume dynasty and turned it into a national success.

But it wasn't enough. It had never been enough—for either of them. There were more successes out there, more opportunities to seize, including their upcoming launch in the States of their newest and finest perfume yet—Valente's Woman. Alex knew his father admired that same drive to conquer in himself. It was part of the reason he'd been tasked with the USA launch.

"And that is…" Alex prompted, leaving the sentence hanging.

"I've come to a decision…" Cesare's pause was surely for effect. "You're thirty-five years old. It's time you married and produced an heir."

Alex felt a brief moment of shock, then his eyes narrowed and his lips twisted. "I'll take your wishes into consideration *if* I ever decide to marry."

"You're not taking me seriously, *figlio mio*," Cesare said, lapsing into Italian to say *son of mine*.

Alex made a sound of derision. "There's a reason for that." He was a Valente, and Valentes didn't like being ordered about. His father knew that.

"I'm very serious about this," Cesare said quietly and firmly. "I'm getting older and I've recently had a…health scare."

Something jolted inside Alex's chest. "You didn't tell me about that."

"No, I didn't." Just for a moment Cesare's eyes clouded over, then cleared. "I was having chest pains. They thought it was a heart attack, but I'm thankful it wasn't. *This* time. It's stress. I have to slow down, but I'm not going to hand over the reins of the business to you until I see you married with an heir on the way."

Alex shot him a withering look. "You're not asking much."

"I'm not asking, Alex. I'm telling. You've got six months in which to find yourself a wife and start a family or…"

Alex's brow winged upward in challenge. "Or?"

"I sell the House of Valente to one of our competitors and give the money to charity. And I promise neither you nor your two brothers will see a cent."

Alex's jaw clenched. "I could always declare you insane."

Cesare gave a small smile. "You could *try* but I don't think any judge will give you power of attorney. I'm as sane as you are and I intend to do what I like with my own company."

Alex swore then pushed to his feet. "I don't need

your money, Dad, nor do I need to be CEO. I'll survive without you."

"But will your brothers?"

Alex's shoulders stiffened. He took his status as eldest brother seriously. His own mother had died when he was three years old and Cesare had married again soon afterward. That marriage had lasted all of a year, just enough time for Nick to be born. Then his father had married Isabel, and had stayed married ever since. Matt at least had both his parents around.

"If you don't do as I ask, then I'll sell tomorrow. You and your brothers will be out on your own."

Alex glared down at him. "We're grown men. We'll survive."

"Oh, I have no doubt about that. But do you think it's fair for them to lose their inheritance like this?"

"Don't manipulate me," Alex growled.

"This isn't manipulation. It's a guarantee," Cesare said with quiet emphasis. "Alex, this is too important to me. It's my legacy to my sons. One day you'll realize this when you have a child of your own."

"Go to hell." Alex strode to the door and closed it behind him with controlled anger. He always wore his detachment like a second skin, but right now he was in danger of losing even that.

One week later

"And now," a woman's well-spoken voice said, "here is Anastasia stepping out for an evening of glamour in a beautiful gown that is sure to make a statement. The plunging neckline…"

Alex heard the female voice through the microphone as he strode along the corridor toward the hotel ballroom. Her tone intrigued him even before he saw the woman, her accent Australian with an American twist, its slightly husky quality entrancing him beyond the beat of the music.

"…and doesn't this set a new style? The classic black is…"

His steps lengthened. He had to see this woman. Had to know if she looked as good as she sounded. He pushed open the door and stepped inside the room, the muted lighting allowing him full view down the well-lit center aisle to the tall, graceful blonde at the podium.

She'd been worth the rush.

Definitely.

Strikingly beautiful, with golden-blond hair pulled back in a sophisticated chignon, she carried an elegance that was as natural as breathing.

There was a round of applause as the model on the runway walked off, and he noticed his stepmother wave to him from the front row. He realized she must have been keeping an eye out for him. He hadn't exactly been enamored of attending a fashion show, but his father had cried off sick at the last minute and Isabel had been persuasive.

He was never more glad he'd agreed to come, he mused, making his way around the edge of the room toward Isabel…toward this beauty on the stage who could have been one of the models herself.

"For our next outfit, Crystal is wearing a jewel of a gown that…"

Just as he reached his stepmother, he looked up at the podium and his eyes locked with those of the blonde. It was a moment out of time.

"Er…" She faltered just that little bit. "…this accents her perfect figure…"

Alex watched her recover and carry on with the commentary, vaguely aware of Isabel's whisper chiding him for being late.

The blonde glanced at him again and he caught a flicker of disconcertion in her eyes before she angled her chin and looked away to continue talking.

But it was too late.

He'd seen her reaction. She'd definitely felt something between them, and if that was panic he'd just seen on her face, then she was panicked by her own emotions.

Good. He wanted this woman, and what he wanted he usually got. Until now he'd been a man who only slept with a woman after he'd gotten to know her, but he'd rethink that tonight. The draw of this woman was too strong.

"And now, one of the highlights of the Cannington Collection is this delightful garment showcasing…"

Alex frowned when he heard the Cannington name but before he could think further, Isabel leaned toward him and whispered, "She's beautiful, isn't she?"

He pretended not to know who she was talking about. "The model?"

Isabel tutted softly. "No, the presenter. She's a famous fashion designer in the States and this is her fashion show. She grew up here and now she's come back to live in Australia. Her mother's Felicia Cannington, you know. The movie star."

Alex let that sink in. Most people knew Felicia Cannington was an Australian who'd made it big in Hollywood over three decades ago. She was a much-loved favorite of the big screen.

He glanced again at the beautiful blonde. "And that's her daughter up there?"

Isabel nodded. "Yes, that's Olivia Cannington."

His business brain kicked into gear and he knew he'd just been handed the perfect solution to his problems. For the last week he'd been thinking about nothing but his father's ultimatum. He'd hoped by now Cesare would admit he'd been totally unreasonable because of his health scare, but the wily old bastard hadn't backed down. When Cesare Valente wanted something he usually got it.

Not that he'd said anything to his father about it. At first he'd been determined not to give in to Cesare's demand and planned on ignoring it as long as he could.

But the guilt had been getting to him. How could he let the family business be handed over to a bunch of strangers? More importantly, how could he let Nick and Matt lose their rightful inheritance?

Now he didn't have to, he decided. He'd grant part of his father's wish *only* because he'd found a suitable woman.

As for producing a child… Cesare could whistle in the dark over that. His father would be retiring within the next couple of months anyway and wouldn't be able to maintain his control over the business. No, a child wouldn't be a part of the bargain.

It would be just him and the blonde. If she was as captivating as she looked, and if she was available, then he'd found the woman to marry.

Olivia Cannington.

* * *

"Good evening, Mr. Valente," Olivia replied with as much cool politeness as she could. She'd recognized Alex Valente's name as soon as her business partner had introduced them. The House of Valente was well-known throughout Australia for its excellence in perfume design and production.

"Alex," he invited, his slate-gray eyes sweeping over her with a burning intensity that made her heart bump against her ribs.

Holding on to her composure, she inclined her head. "Alex." She ignored the meaningful look Lianne gave her before the other woman excused herself and took off across the room to see to their other guests.

Instead, she let a moment pass as she took a sip of her champagne and tried not to show how much this handsome man affected her.

Darn him. The party after the show was usually a lighthearted affair, with everyone relaxed and ready to enjoy themselves after all the hard work they'd put in to make the collection a success.

But Alex Valente had spoiled the whole thing for her tonight. From the moment he'd stepped into the ballroom he'd caught her attention. It was an attention she didn't welcome or need, but he'd been staring at her so hard during the show she'd lost her focus. It had unnerved her, making her stumble over her words. That had never happened to her before.

So she wasn't particularly happy about meeting him now. "Did you enjoy the show?" For all his sophistication, she suspected he was more at home working in his office than attending a fashion show.

"It was…fascinating."

"Do you often go to fashion shows?" she asked, making small talk, passing the time, hearing the chatter going on around them, the music getting louder.

A wry smile entered his eyes. "No. I only came to accompany my stepmother."

Olivia remembered seeing the elegant woman sitting next to him. "I see. Did she stay for the party? Is she here now?" Perhaps he'd go find her and not come back. She silently sighed. That was about as likely as the moon turning to cheese.

"No, my father wasn't feeling well tonight so she decided to go home."

"I hope he's okay."

Alex's mouth tightened. "He is."

She considered his words. "You sound certain about that."

"My father's very good at getting his own way," he said brusquely.

"I have a mother who's the same," she joked in a

moment of empathy, then regretted allowing any cor-relation between her and Alex.

He didn't smile.

There was a tiny pause. Then, "God, you're beautiful."

She blinked, hardening her heart as it bounced inside her chest. "Oh, puh-lease."

His jaw clenched. "Don't prejudge me, Olivia. I don't need to flatter to get my way. If I like some-thing, I say so. If I want something, I ask."

"Or take," she said, her lip curling, instinctively knowing what sort of man he was. Yes, he was a taker. One who'd take a woman to the heights, then down to the very depths of her being.

"See," he mocked. "You know me already."

She drew her shoulders back. "Mr. Valente—"

"Alex."

"Alex, look. I don't mean to be rude, but—"

"I have a proposition for you."

Shocked, she still managed to shoot him a with-ering look. "That figures."

An icy glint appeared in his eyes. "That's quite an attitude you've got there."

She suddenly felt defensive. "It's justified."

A moment crept by. "So every person you meet is judged by one criterion, are they?"

His question made her angry. He must be intelligent enough to know that all her life people had used her to get to her mother. And now they used her in her own right. Not that it got them very far these days.

Not after Eric.

What a fool she'd been for marrying such a liar and a cheat. Five years ago she'd been twenty-two and unprepared for his lesson in deception. Little had she known he'd wanted her for her money, until he'd found another woman with even more money and had run off with her.

Her chin lifted. "Mr. Valente, if all this is leading somewhere, please tell me where."

"Dinner."

Her heart thudded once. "What about it?"

"Have dinner with me tomorrow night."

Her heart thudded twice. "I can't."

He met her gaze for long seconds. "You have another engagement?"

"No."

There was a slight lifting of his brow. "Then why not have dinner with me?"

She hated this interrogation. "How do you know I'm not involved with someone?"

"If you are, I feel sorry for him. I wouldn't like it

if *my* woman was attracted to another man the way you are to me."

She sucked in a lungful of air. "Don't be ridiculous. I'm not attracted to you."

He raised his brows.

"Look, I'm sure any other woman would be only too glad to go out with you." She drew herself up taller. "Please excuse me, now." With that, she walked away with her back straight and her head held high and let herself be swallowed up in the crowd.

She half expected him to follow her, but after that he seemed to have disappeared. She was glad, she told herself. She already had a headache from the music that was getting progressively louder.

Going out for dinner with a man like Alex Valente would not be prudent, she knew. She already had enough disasters to deal with—she wouldn't add possible heartache to the list.

Two

The next day Olivia was in her office when a courier delivered a letter for her marked Personal.

There was just something about that strong handwriting that put her on alert. She gazed down at the white envelope in her hand, noting the way her name had been written in bold strokes. Her heart skipped a beat. Was she being silly to think this was from Alex Valente?

It was.

It read, *Dinner tonight. Seven-thirty. Sylvester's Restaurant.*

She stared at the note, her blood pressure beginning to rise. The sheer arrogance of the man! He sure
didn't take no for an answer.

Heavens, just the thought of spending an evening
with Alex Valente was enough to give her a serious
case of goose bumps. She couldn't deny she was
deeply attracted to him. There was a strength about
him that appealed to her.

Of course that was probably because the men in her
life had always been weak in some way or other. Her
parents had divorced when she was two, and her father
had ignored her for most of her life. Her successive two
stepfathers had both been kind but self-centered. And
her ex-husband had only been interested in himself.
They hadn't been good examples of the male species.

So why did she think Alex Valente *was?*

By six that evening she knew she would meet
him. She had too much to worry about these days and
wondering what Alex wanted from her did not need
to be added to her list.

At least the restaurant was neutral ground, she
told herself, showering then dressing in one of her
own classic designs. The cream-colored pantsuit flat-
tered her tall slim figure. Matching leather pumps
completed a sophisticated but businesslike effect.

She might as well have worn nothing, she mused

an hour later. Alex had watched her entrance into the restaurant with a masculine appreciation that sent a tingle of anticipation along her spine.

"Glad you could make it," he said, his voice low and throaty as she reached the corner table.

"*I'm* not," she said, then quickly cleared the huskiness from her throat.

A knowing look entered his eyes. "So why did you come?"

She angled her chin at him. "To tell you that I found your note arrogant and to make it clear I want nothing to do with you."

"You could have just phoned and said the same thing."

"But would you have given up?"

He arched a brow. "Do I look like a man who gives up?"

"No."

"Then you have your answer." He held out her chair for her. "Let's eat first."

She swallowed. First? She didn't much feel like eating, but the waiter was hovering, so she went through the motions and ordered a glass of mineral water, then glanced at the menu and ordered veal.

"You've obviously done some checking to find me," she said, once they were alone.

"I needed to get the note to you," he dismissed, as if checking up on people was what he did every day.

Well, she'd done some checking herself this afternoon, but she wasn't about to tell him that. She'd heard of the House of Valente—who hadn't? But until now she'd never been interested in reading the odd gossip column about the love exploits of the three Valente brothers.

"Alex, I—"

"I love your name," he cut across her, his voice suddenly deepening to a murmur. *"Olivia."*

Her heart fluttered at the sound of her name on his lips. He made it sound so sexy…so downright delicious…so….

All at once she realized what he was doing and her mouth tightened. He obviously liked to interrupt her with a personal comment just to throw her off-balance.

"I was named after Larry," she told him, hiding a smirk.

His brow arched. "Larry?"

"Sir Laurence Olivier. You know, the actor."

His hard, sensual mouth visibly relaxed. "Oh. I know who he is. Or was."

She emphasized a sigh. "Alas, he died before I was born, but he was like a favorite uncle to my mother."

Alex's eyes held amusement. "I can see you're trying to put me in my place."

An odd exhilaration filled her. "Did it work?"

"No. But then, I have friends in high places, too. And they're all still alive." One corner of his mouth twisted upward. "I'd say you've tried that little trick before."

"Not since I was a teenager. I've grown up since then."

"And very nicely, too," he drawled.

While the waiter was placing their drinks on the table, Olivia couldn't help but take a proper look at Alex from beneath her lashes. Lord. The man was handsome to a fault, his dark looks a lethal combination of virility and commanding self-confidence, the superbly tailored suit he wore merely an excuse to take a second look at him.

Then she noticed he'd seen her assessing him. Her cheeks warmed as her heart tried to settle. She was grateful when he started to discuss less personal things and Olivia felt herself relax as the conversation stayed on general topics.

"Are you close to your mother, Olivia?" he said, just after the waiter took away their empty plates.

Uneasiness sliced through her. "Why do you ask?"

"You were raised by your grandmother here in

Australia, weren't you? Your mother lived in Los Angeles." He made it sound as if her mother had deserted her.

"It wasn't like that," she said, defensively. "My mother's work was in Los Angeles. She thought I'd have a better upbringing with my grandmother and I did. Nanna and I loved each other." Her heart squeezed at the thought of her grandmother's passing seven years ago.

All at once she realized she was justifying her family. "Look, why did you invite me here, Alex?"

"Because you need me."

She almost choked. "Excuse me?"

He sent her a mocking look. "Let me put it another way. You need my money."

She suddenly felt a chill. Could he know about her mother's debts? It had to be the best-kept secret in LA, but only because she worked hard to earn the money to keep up her mother's normally elaborate lifestyle.

Oh God. Could Alex actually know something about her mother? If he did, would he use that knowledge? If rumors started that her mother was in debt up to her neck, her mother's career, already on a downhill slide, could be all but over.

Her mother would never survive the humiliation.

She needed to play this cool. "I don't know what you mean. Why would *I* need your money?"

"Your business is floundering, Olivia. You and your partner overextended by opening boutiques in Sydney, Brisbane and Melbourne and now you're in debt. You should have just started with the Sydney one."

She let out a slow breath of relief. So, he didn't know about her mother at all. Thank heavens!

And funny, but she was pleased to hear his opinion. It had been her intention to open one boutique at a time but Lianne had persuaded her otherwise, her partner thinking it was a great idea to go for three at once.

And it would have been if all their clients had paid them the money they owed.

Naturally the fashion show had put them further in the red. As had another of her mother's lavish parties put together as a means to help her get a part in a movie that now wasn't even getting made.

"You need cash to get your business out of trouble," Alex continued, bringing her mind back to their conversation.

She shrugged. "It's a temporary cash flow problem, that's all."

"You're an exceptional fashion designer, Olivia,

but that won't save your business. You need money and you need it quickly."

"I can get the money if I want. I have connections." And the minute she used them, her boutiques would no longer be her own.

"So why haven't you used those connections before now? You're leaving it a bit late."

She picked up her glass of mineral water and took a sip, giving herself time to reply. "Pride, I guess. I don't like owing anything to anyone. But if it comes to the crunch, I'll swallow my pride if I have to."

A long moment crept by, then, "Marry me, Olivia, and I promise you won't owe a thing."

She gave herself a mental shake. "Excuse me?"

"Marry me."

She laughed as she put down her glass. "You're delusional."

Challenge flared in his eyes. "Far from it."

This was absolutely crazy. She'd only just met the man. Did he even know the type of person she was? Did he care?

"I'm attracted to you," he said, his gaze dropping to her mouth as if he was tempted to kiss her. "And you're attracted to me. You felt it as soon as we first saw each other."

"The only thing I'm feeling is disbelief. And anger." A woman would have to be desperate to marry a stranger, much less marry a man like Alex Valente. He had to be kidding.

A look of implacable determination crossed his face. "What's that perfume you're wearing?"

She stared at him, baffled at the change in subject. "You must know what it is. It's Valente's Woman."

"So you like it then?" He didn't give her time to answer. "Or did you wear it just for me tonight?" he asked, his voice taking on a husky quality that shivered through her.

She ignored that shiver. "No, I didn't wear it just for you tonight. It happens to be a gorgeous scent and I love it. I wear it all the time." And that was the truth.

He inclined his head, his eyes turning business-like. "And so do most women in Australia."

"I'm sure you're right." This particular perfume called to something inside her. It possessed a fascinating quality and retained a sensual edge that, to her mind, made it the perfect perfume. She rather thought she'd like to wear it for the rest of her life.

"We're about to launch it in the States in a big way," he said, drawing her from her thoughts. "And I've come to a decision. We can use all the publicity we can get, but I can't think of any better publicity than the CEO of the House of Valente marrying someone with the famous Cannington name."

She was so shocked at his reasoning, it took her a moment to think past what he was saying.

And then a derisive sound escaped her mouth. "Let me get this right. You'll pay me to marry you for the sake of a *perfume?*"

"Why not? I've heard of worse reasons. And while it's too late for the launch right now, we could eventually promote the perfume along with your line of fashion." He leaned back comfortably in his chair and took another sip of his Scotch. "Marry me and I'll pay all your debts."

Pay her debts? Plus the chance to combine the Valente perfume and her fashion designs? The thought of it intrigued her.

Then she realized she was actually thinking about it. Good grief! There was no way she was going to consider marrying a man for money. No way at all.

Her hand tightened around her glass. "As delightful as your offer sounds," she said with sarcasm, "I really can't accept it."

His gaze penetrated to the bone. "You're between a rock and a hard place. How else will you get the money?"

"Perhaps I'll go to the newspapers and sell them a story. I'm sure they'd be *very* interested in your offer."

His look was of faint amusement. "But then I'd have to tell them about your financial crisis. And I'm sure they'd be equally as interested in that, if not more."

Damn him. She had to protect her mother, especially now, when Felicia badly needed to get her career back on track. After all, the one time she'd really needed her mother, Felicia had been there for her, helping her through the divorce. Not to mention, her mother had given her money to help start up her fashion design business in the first place.

But as Olivia looked at Alex, her brow crinkled in a frown. What was this actually about? What was his reasoning behind it all? A man like Valente didn't need to marry *her*. His own family had plenty of wealth and privilege. She couldn't see how Valente's Woman could possibly fail in America. Not with Alex Valente running the show.

She tilted her head and considered him. "There's more to your offer than you're saying."

Wary surprise flickered in his eyes. He took a sip of his Scotch before answering. "That's very perceptive of you. You're a sharp lady."

Her heart gave a little flutter at the compliment. "This isn't about me," she reminded him.

Sudden tension tautened the hard line of his shoulders. "My father thinks it's time I married. He says he'll sell the business and give the proceeds all away to charity if I don't, and neither of my two brothers nor myself will get a cent."

She blinked in shock. This man would hate to be told what to do. "That seems rather drastic."

"My father never does anything in half measures," he said, somewhat cynically. "He's being forced to retire for health reasons, and he's tasked me with the American launch. I expect he'll want me to take over as head of the company, only he won't do that until I'm settled."

"So you're after your father's approval then?" she said, somewhat surprised by the thought. Not that there was anything wrong with wanting a parent's approval. It was just that Alex seemed too independent, too remote to worry about what anyone else thought.

Not a flicker of emotion crossed his face. "No, I couldn't care less about his approval," he said, confirming her intuition. "This is for the sake of the company and for my two younger brothers."

She frowned. "It's a big request."

His mouth set in a stubborn line. "I've decided to play along for a year."

"So our marriage wouldn't be permanent then?"

"No."

This was beginning to sound much more favorable. "And we wouldn't be sleeping together?"

The corner of his lips curved up, yet his eyes
darkened. "This isn't make-believe, Olivia. It would
be a real marriage."

Her stomach flipped at the thought of them in
bed together.

Making love together.

Feeling flushed, she had to drag her eyes away
from him…then back. "If the Cannington name is all
you want, you could always marry my mother," she
joked, but instantly regretted it. Her mother was still
a beautiful woman. And she'd been married three
times already.

His gaze strayed over her. "No. You're the one I
want."

His comment snatched her breath away. With a
supreme effort, she mentally fought to put up a wall.
"I've been married before, you know."

His eyes narrowed. "I know."

Panic rose in her throat. She couldn't do it. No, not
for the business. Not for her mother. Not even for a
year. The heartache had been too much last time.

Somehow she managed to get a grip. "But I'm
divorced. Doesn't that make me less than perfect?"

she said, giving him an out, putting a stop to all this craziness. She had to.

Someone had to.

A frown creased the skin between his brows. "No, it doesn't."

A warm feeling bounced inside her chest, but she tried to stay strong. "I swore I'd never marry again."

His eyes took on a softer look. "This wouldn't be for love, Olivia. You wouldn't have to worry about me hurting you."

She wasn't so sure about that. Heartache and marriage usually went together. It had happened in her mother's three marriages, and in her own one.

Alex placed his half-empty glass on the table. "I'll give you twenty-four hours to think things over."

"How generous," she quipped. Somehow she didn't think a lifetime was enough to think things over with this man.

"Be home tomorrow night. I'll drop by your apartment."

"Or you could just phone me," she mocked, using the same comment he'd used when she'd first arrived.

"No chance. I'm not letting you escape."

Her chin lifted. "You may not have a choice."

"You may not either."

Just then the waiter returned and she bit her lip to stop from making a remark. Fine. She'd allow him the last word.

This time.

Olivia spent a restless night thinking over Alex's offer, trying to decide whether she needed to take the drastic action of marrying a man for money. One minute she convinced herself she could do it, then she couldn't. She would, then she wouldn't.

Heavens, if it'd just been for the business's sake she'd dismiss it out of hand and take her chances with a bank. But the opportunity to earn some money without needing to pay it back, and without needing to explain why half of that money needed to go to her mother, was sobering.

Yet marriage?

She couldn't.

And then she reminded herself how her mother had helped her through the divorce. Shattered by Eric's betrayal, the last thing Olivia had expected was that her mother would bring her back home to Australia for a few months to recover. Olivia wouldn't forget her mother being there for her.

But marriage to Alex? Dear Lord, she wasn't sure she could ever learn to trust another man.

She froze. Or did she really need to worry about trust? Alex *had* said it wasn't a love match, so at least he was being upfront about it.

The next evening she opened her apartment door to him with a noncommittal expression, but her pulse had quickened. There was no doubt he affected her. Everything about him suggested an intense and indelible masculinity that made her tingle.

This isn't make-believe, Olivia. It would be a real marriage.

She swallowed hard and closed the door behind him. "Would you like a drink?"

He stood a few feet away in the open-plan living room. "What do you have?"

She pasted on a false smile. "Prune juice?"

He gave a husky chuckle. "Coffee if you have it."

"I do." She went to turn toward the kitchen.

"Remember those words."

She stopped with a frown. "What do you—" She realized what he meant. "Oh."

"They sound perfect for a wedding ceremony, don't you think?" His eyes were watchful.

But she wasn't about to give him the satisfaction of telling him her decision yet. Let him wait. He had to learn he couldn't always get his own way. Or control people. Not *her* anyway.

She turned and walked into the kitchen, then glanced up to see him following her. Ignoring him, she reached for the coffeepot but could feel his eyes looking around the apartment then on her, no doubt comparing her modest surroundings to a Hollywood lifestyle.

Only she couldn't explain that she lived modestly for a reason. That she'd been paying her mother's debts off these past few years. Anyway, this was no hardship. She'd been mostly raised by her grandmother here in Sydney in a comfortable suburban house, far from the excesses of LA.

"You enjoy being a fashion designer?"

She poured the coffee into two mugs. "Yes. I wouldn't do it otherwise."

"You never wanted to be a movie star like your mother?"

She passed him a mug. "I can't act."

He casually leaned against the door frame. "So it doesn't run in the blood then?"

"I'm a simple girl at heart," she half joked, then rested against the kitchen counter and looked at him over the top of her mug. "If you're expecting more then you're going to be disappointed."

His gaze lingered on her. "No, I don't think I will be," he murmured, making the breath hitch in her throat.

"I—" She wasn't even sure what she was going to say. Something…anything…to stop the overwhelming need to step into his arms. "This is crazy," she said.

"No, it isn't."

Realizing she was giving away too much of what she was feeling, she swung around and placed her coffee mug in the sink. Taking a calming breath, she turned back to meet his eyes. "Alex, look—"

"What's your decision, Olivia?"

"I'll marry you," she said, seeing his eyes flare with satisfaction—mixed with something else. "On one condition. You give me half the money now."

Whatever that something else was that she'd seen lurking in his eyes disappeared. He gave a hard laugh as he put his mug down on the table. "I'm a businessman, Olivia. I'm not about to give you any money before you marry me."

She felt a spurt of anger. "My word isn't good enough?"

Irritation swept over his face. "Look, this isn't about your word. It's not personal. This is a business decision."

"Not personal? You want me to marry you and share your bed and you say it's not personal?" Her brow arched. "Just when *does* it get personal, Alex?"

His jaw set but he acknowledged her words with a nod. "Okay, I concede the point."

Olivia met his gaze levelly. "Then we have an agreement?"

A brief hesitation as he scrutinized her, then, "Yes."

Relief swept through her. Relief she would get the money, not relief she was marrying him, she told herself. "Good."

For a moment she wondered if she should tell him about her mother's money problems. Could she trust him? No. She didn't know him at all. Besides, it was her mother's secret.

As for her own secret, she'd never tell him about that. She wouldn't *have* to tell him about it, considering the briefness of their upcoming marriage.

Suddenly he was all business. "Can you be ready in two weeks' time?"

Her mouth dropped open. "*Two* weeks?"

"We have to do this as soon as possible. I've already booked the Sydney Opera House for the ceremony."

She swallowed, ignoring for the moment that the Opera House was one of the most beautiful venues in the world. "You were *that* certain of me?"

"Yes."

"You're an arrogant bastard."

"I believe you've mentioned that already," he drawled.

"I can't possibly be ready in two weeks' time. I'm off to LA in a couple of days. I promised my mother I would visit with her. She hasn't been feeling very well lately."

And that was an understatement. Her mother knew she couldn't continue with her lavish parties and her high maintenance. She knew it was coming to an end unless she found herself a major role.

All at once Alex looked thoughtful. "You know something. This could play in our favor. If you keep a low profile while you're over there, it will add to the mystique of our wedding."

Our wedding.

She sent him a cynical look. "Yes, and we definitely want mystique for those perfume sales, don't we?"

He glanced at her oddly, as if it was a given. "It'll help your sales as well."

Okay, so he was right. But getting her mother to keep a low profile when the media were bound to be knocking at their door? Impossible! Of course, using Alex's "mystique" angle might be the way to go. Felicia loved "mystique." She knew the value of it.

"What about your father?" Alex asked, drawing her from her thoughts. "Do you want him at the wedding?"

An old heartache jarred but she quickly stomped

on it. "No. He lives in Vancouver with his family and I have little to do with him."

He nodded with a grimace. "Some men don't know when they've got a good thing."

She shrugged. "Owen Cannington was a B-grade actor who gave it all up years ago. He divorced my mother when I was two."

"She kept his name," he pointed out.

"Only because she was becoming well-known as Felicia Cannington." Her lips twisted. "Mum said she may as well make some use of him."

"Sounds like the divorce was amicable," he mocked.

She couldn't help herself. She had to smile, if only the tiniest one she could find.

Taking her by surprise, Alex was suddenly in front of her, putting his hand under her chin. She started to speak, but his mouth closed over hers, holding her there beneath him, taking without asking, as if it was his right.

And then his tongue dipped inside her mouth and did a sweep, exploring her, getting to know her, until she shuddered from a flood of sensation that shook her world.

He eased back, his eyes dark with a passion that didn't surprise her at all. "There," he murmured huskily. "At least that's one thing we've got out of the way."

She swallowed hard. "Um…I didn't know it was *in* the way."

He arched a mocking brow before leaving. They both knew she was lying, if even to herself.

Three

Alex watched Olivia walk toward him in her wedding gown. The white, off-the-shoulder, satin dress was slim and elegant, and it looked absolutely stunning on her. How had he not known she existed before this? he wondered, filled with a deep satisfaction that he'd found the woman he'd wanted for his temporary wife.

God, she was beautiful.

Beautiful and lovely and so very picture-perfect.

Surprisingly he'd missed her these last two weeks and had actually been pleased to see her when she'd arrived back in the country only forty-eight hours ago.

There'd been a hell of a lot to do with a high-profile wedding such as theirs, the time having gone fast, though not fast enough for his peace of mind. He'd wanted this marriage signed and sealed and he wanted Olivia Cannington in his bed. Just the thought of making her *his* sent the blood rushing through him.

Right then she reached him and their eyes met for one long moment before they turned toward the female marriage celebrant.

The ceremony began, and through the huge window in front of them, they could see the sun shine on the spectacular backdrop of the famous Sydney Harbour Bridge suspended over vibrant blue water dotted with sails.

They exchanged traditional wedding vows, and Alex felt a twinge of guilt when he promised "to cherish her until death do us part." He would have liked to change the vows to "to have and to hold for as long as they both stayed married." Only he didn't want to think about divorce on their wedding day.

Then suddenly their marriage was a fact and he was told he could kiss the bride.

With pleasure.

Soft pink colored Olivia's cheeks as he leaned toward her. Seeing her eyes drop to his mouth sent something powerful flaring inside him. He placed his lips against hers for a long moment that wasn't wholly for the benefit of their guests.

Tonight there would be no audience….

Soon they stood on the steps of the Opera House, where it seemed the world's media wanted to take their picture.

Not that he minded, usually. He'd grown up in the Australian spotlight, but this was different. One part of him felt a wedding day should be private, yet another part was gratified he'd done the right thing in using this avenue to highlight Valente's Woman.

"Can we have a photograph of you and Olivia looking deep into each other's eyes?"

He glanced at Olivia with a sideways smile. "Can we do that?"

She gave a tight smile. "Yes, I think we can," she said, but only he could see her eyes were guarded as he turned to stare into them.

"You're doing fine," he murmured, noticing the flecks of different shades of blue that sparkled in her eyes.

She winced a little. "This is hard work."

"Just pretend you love me," he drawled, attempting to put her at ease.

A genuine smile tilted the corners of her mouth. "It would be easier if I didn't hate you so much."

He chuckled and cameras snapped all around them, and he realized being joined in holy matrimony with Olivia was going to be more than interesting. She was a challenge. And he liked challenges.

"Can we have a picture of you both with the bride's mother?"

Alex felt Olivia stiffen beside him and that reminded him of last night's dinner. She'd seemed edgy around Felicia, as though she expected her mother to take center stage all the time.

And of course "the star" had done exactly that, he remembered with mild amusement. The older woman was elegant and charming, and he could easily see where Olivia got those same qualities from.

Yet he sensed Felicia had an emotional fragility about her that Olivia didn't. Perhaps that's what made Felicia such a good actress, he mused, as she came forward and smiled at the cameras like the pro she was.

"Felicia, how does it feel to be the mother of the bride?" one of the journalists called out.

"Old," she said with a pout.

Everyone chuckled. "You're not so old, Felicia," the journalist said.

Felicia sent him a stunning movie-star smile.

"Darling, I love you." She winked. "Come and see me after the reception."

"I'll hold you to that," the reporter quipped with a huge grin.

Felicia chuckled, stepping between Olivia and Alex and linking her arms through theirs. "Let's smile for the cameras, darlings."

A few minutes later, they were *still* snapping pictures. Alex looked across at Olivia and could see how much of a strain it was becoming. He felt the same. On the other hand, Felicia seemed as though she would go on forever, cornering the attention and loving it all. It's what she did best.

He stepped away from the women. "Right, that's enough," he all but growled. They still had a reception to get through.

Felicia darted a look at him and seemed to realize the moment was over. She turned back to the cameras and clapped her hands. "Right, fellas. That's a wrap. This is my daughter's day and I want to go play mother of the bride."

Alex looked beyond the words and realized something. He had no doubt Felicia loved her daughter, but he had to wonder if Felicia didn't love Felicia just that little bit more. He suddenly had a new appreciation of what it must be like to live with a superstar.

And he had a new appreciation of Olivia as her own person. For Olivia to get out from under her mother's shadow, to make a name for herself as she'd done, showed her depth of character. He'd chosen well in his bride.

Hell, and he'd just gotten married!

His sacrifice had been worth it.

Then he looked at his new wife and all at once it didn't seem like such a sacrifice. There would be benefits.

Very nice benefits.

Not the least of which would be making love to a flawless beauty who put up walls he now intended to pull down.

Olivia was glad when they moved back inside the Opera House to the waiting reception. Not that she had escaped the prying eyes. There were at least three hundred guests here today and the haste of their marriage had most of them looking at her and Alex with suspicion.

Was she or wasn't she?

It was a thought she tried to put to the side and not think about. It had been the same last night at a Valente family dinner in her honor. She couldn't help but note the question in everyone's eyes.

Everyone's except Cesare Valente's.

He knew why Alex was marrying her so hastily.

Surprisingly, Olivia hadn't expected to like Alex's father, but she did. And his stepmother, Isabel, was a doll. Both his parents hit it off really well with Felicia, and Isabel had even promised to keep an eye on Felicia until her mother returned to the States in a week's time. Her mother was such a good actress that a week of being charming to people who were charmed by her shouldn't be so difficult.

As for herself, she hadn't realized how much of an actress she was until today. As she danced with Alex, she tried not to let everyone see how much he affected her. And *he* knew it, too. That confident, arrogant gleam in his eyes told her how *much* he knew it with every step they took.

"You look beautiful in that wedding dress," he murmured, sending her heart pounding like a hammer.

"Thank you."

"Was it something you just threw together?" he teased.

Her lips twitched. "Actually I designed it for the daughter of a billionaire, but the wedding was called off at the last minute so I got to keep the dress."

"I hope they paid you for it."

She glanced away then back again. "We're still

working on that." The father was being obstructive, which no doubt accounted for his billions.

Alex frowned. "Let me know if you need any help."

Olivia couldn't help it. She chuckled. "What are you going to do? Set the dogs on him?"

He grinned. "I could rough him up a little for you."

She laughed again and his grin widened. Maybe it was from being whirled around the dance floor, but all at once she felt giddy—giddy with the pleasure of looking at him. Seconds ticked by, and the gleam in his eyes told her he felt something, too.

The music ended, giving her the chance to move out of his arms. Soon they stood talking to his two brothers and Olivia tried to look calm.

"How's it feel to be an old married man now, Alex?" Nick Valente teased, his lips curved in a confident smile that must be a family trait.

Alex slid his arm around Olivia, pulling her close to smile down at her. "Can you blame me for wanting to tie the knot with this beauty?"

She felt herself flush, but drew her gaze away from Alex and found both Nick and Matt considering her with piercing eyes.

"No," Matt drawled. "I can't say I blame you at all."

Olivia stared at all three men. *Handsome* was too tame a word for them. Yet it was more than just looks. It was an innate quality. They were men who knew who they were and what they wanted. Nothing would stop them.

She wondered if they suspected the sacrifice their older brother had made for them. Alex had told her they didn't know about his father's demand, but she wasn't so sure they didn't suspect something. It was there in the way both men looked at her, as if they didn't trust any woman or her motives, and especially when that woman had hooked one of them in marriage.

Thankfully, Isabel came up to them with Cesare, sniffing back tears in an elegant manner. "Cesare, I can't believe our eldest boy is now married."

Olivia knew that Isabel was Alex's stepmother, not his real mother, who had died when he was small, but by all accounts he considered Isabel his "true" mother.

Cesare glanced at Alex then away again. "Izzie, he's a grown man, not a boy," he said, a hint of gruffness in his voice that made Olivia look at him and wonder if he regretted forcing his son into this marriage. A moment later she came up against a new, determined look in the older man's eyes that said his moment of regret had passed.

"Oh, Cesare," Isabel lightly scolded. "I'm allowed to be sentimental today. I'm the mother of the groom." She hugged Olivia. "And I have a beautiful daughter now, too," she said, sending a warmth through Olivia that made her suddenly want to cry.

"Pity I didn't see her first," Nick joked, giving Olivia a slow wink.

"It wouldn't have mattered," Alex said, pulling her in even closer against his hip, his voice totally serious. "She was mine from the moment I saw her."

She gasped, even as Nick stared at Alex and held his gaze. Then whatever he saw had the middle brother nodding in agreement. "I believe you're right."

Olivia's moment of warmth disappeared but before she could take them to task for their comment, Isabel said, "Stop it, you two. You're embarrassing Olivia."

But Olivia wasn't embarrassed.

She was angry.

It was bad enough knowing she'd walked into this marriage with her eyes open, but making her sound as if she was something to be tossed back and forth between the brothers didn't make her feel exactly civil toward them.

As if Isabel knew, she clicked her tongue and slipped her arm through Olivia's, drawing her away from Alex. "Come on, sweetie. Let's go see your mother. She'll be missing you."

Olivia gladly let herself be taken away, but a few steps on, Isabel squeezed her arm. "Take no notice of them, Olivia. They're fine men who get a bit carried away with their own self-importance at times." She laughed lightly. "Their father's the same."

Olivia found herself smiling back. It was good to know Isabel understood. This Valente woman knew how to keep her man in line.

Then she realized *she* was one of the Valente women now. Would she be able to keep Alex in line? Unlikely. She'd probably go mad in the attempt.

Hours later Olivia had changed out of her wedding finery into a soft-pink suit. Alex had also changed out of his tuxedo into dark trousers and a sports jacket. Then they said their goodbyes, hopped in a limousine and headed for the airport, where a private jet would fly them up along the coast far north of Sydney to the Valente holiday home near Ballina.

"So," Alex said, once they were in the air and comfortable on the luxurious leather chairs opposite each other. "You enjoyed our wedding?"

She gave a polite smile. "The venue was perfect. Thank you."

"You were wrong about not being able to act. You did well."

Her smile widened with self-derision. "Perhaps I should become an actress after all?"

His face closed up, his jaw clenching. "*After* our marriage is over. Not before."

"I'm not sure your brothers were fooled."

"Even if they suspected something, I won't be telling." Tension suddenly filled the air. "I suggest you stay away from them as much as possible."

If they'd been a normal married couple she'd think he was a little jealous of her spending time with his brothers. As it was, it sounded as if he was just being possessive of her. She was *his* now.

Her lips tightened. "I don't plan on spending any more time with your brothers than necessary."

"Good."

Their gazes held for a brief moment before she turned to look out the window. All at once she felt tired. The last thing she remembered was how exhausted she felt by everything.

She woke to find Alex leaning forward, his warm hand clasping her knee, gently shaking her awake. "We're almost there," he murmured, his eyes a dark smoky gray, his touch a caress that radiated upward along her thigh.

Quickly she pretended he wasn't having an effect on her, but that was like pretending he didn't exist. He *did* exist, and so did his touch. And knowing he'd been watching her sleep…

She shifted and he dropped his hand. "I hope I wasn't sleeping with my mouth open," she said, trying to keep things light.

He leaned back in his chair with a masculine smile that smoldered with awareness. "I'll let you know tomorrow if you snore," he drawled, his gaze dropping to the white camisole she wore beneath her jacket.

She could feel her nipples tighten and her cheeks heat up. "I've been told I don't." There!

His smile disappeared. His eyes flicked out the plane's window then back. "We'll be landing soon. Do you want to freshen up? There's bound to be a photographer or two at the airport." He sounded detached now.

She groaned inwardly, not wanting to be on show anymore today. "Didn't they get enough pictures at the wedding?"

He shrugged.

She gave a nod of acceptance then stood, unnecessarily smoothing her skirt. "I'd better go make myself presentable."

"You're more than presentable," he said, a throaty quality to his voice that made her want to break into a run.

Make that a sprint, she decided, ignoring Alex's gaze down the length of her back as she calmly made her way to the bathroom. Once inside she collapsed back against the door. Whoever said love made the world go round hadn't got it right. It was more sexual attraction that did that.

The sunset was beautiful as they departed the jet, but Olivia barely had time to notice as they walked through some camera flashes to another waiting limousine. She usually wasn't unnerved by the media, but right now she was. At the wedding it had been different.

Less personal.

Now she suddenly felt off-balance and—dare she think it—out of her depth with everything. It was bad enough that Alex probably guessed how she was feeling, but she didn't want the world to know it, too.

Twenty minutes later they drove along a winding road to a floodlit mansion. Set in a lush sub-tropical garden, the two-story house had wide verandas surrounding both top and bottom levels. Palms swayed in the light breeze off the crystal waters and tapped against the louvered-glass windows that covered most of the house.

An older Australian couple greeted them at the door to welcome them to Villa Valente and then Alex suggested she retire to the main suite where they would eat a late dinner.

"I have a couple of calls to make first. I'll join you in about half an hour."

She nodded with relief, looking forward to having some time alone as she followed Harriet up the stairs. They had a minor discussion about the wedding, and the older woman, who seemed very nice, showed her around the deluxe suite, which included a small intimate table set for two in the corner.

There was a pale-blue silk gown and matching robe draped on the king-size bed. "Is this from Alex?" Olivia asked, carefully keeping her voice blank, not sure if she liked him buying her clothes. It smacked too much of proprietorship.

"No. It's a wedding gift from Martin and me." Harriet's face softened. "I know you're a wonderful fashion designer, Mrs. Valente, but I thought you might like this as a personal gift from us. You don't have to wear it tonight if you don't want to."

Olivia relaxed with a smile. "It's lovely, thank you. And yes, I *will* wear it tonight."

"It's our pleasure." Harriet walked to the door. "Let me know if you need anything else."

Olivia nodded, but as the door closed she looked down at the bridal lingerie that was even more glamorous than that she'd planned on wearing for Alex, the outfit he would take off her slowly and seductively, or perhaps in a hurry. She trembled with fear—not of him physically hurting her—but of him physically *knowing* her body.

But, she reminded herself, she'd married Alex today. She'd made a promise to be his wife.

When she came out of the bathroom after showering, the man himself was standing near the table. He'd obviously showered in another bathroom then changed into gray trousers and a black polo shirt that made him look drop-dead handsome.

Heat flared in his eyes. "I didn't think you could get more beautiful," he rasped. "But you are."

Giving an inner moan at the way she dissolved at his words, she shrugged. "Harriet and Martin bought it for me," she said quickly, not wanting him to think she'd dressed like this totally for *him*. "I couldn't *not* wear it."

He held her gaze a moment more. "They have good taste."

She stepped forward, looking at the table. "Speaking of taste, this all looks very delicious."

He waited until she was closer then held out a chair for her. "Yes, it does. Nothing but the best for—"

"A Valente?" she quipped, taking a seat.

"I was going to say for *you*," he murmured near her ear.

"Oh." He was close behind her. She expected his hands to slide over her shoulders and she tensed, preparing for it, almost *wanting* it. But that was only because she *wanted* to get this out of the way, she told herself when he sat down opposite and passed her a glass of wine.

His glass clinked intimately against hers. "To us."

She held his gaze, feeling herself flush. "To us."

They both took a sip from their drinks, then Alex placed his glass on the table. "Now, what would you like to try first?" he drawled, a roguish glint entering his eyes.

She swallowed hard and tried to act sophisticated. Was he suggesting she try him?

Heavens, if he expected her to take the lead then he was in for a shock. There wasn't a woman alive who wouldn't like to make love to him, including herself, but tonight she couldn't quite bring herself to make the first move. She just wasn't sexually experienced enough to be blasé about all this.

She swallowed past her dry throat. "The seafood salad looks nice."

He shot her a knowing look. "Yes," was all he said, then gestured for them to start helping themselves.

After that they ate and made idle conversation about the house, the weather, the food. It wasn't a getting-to-know-you time but more a staving off of the inevitable—at least, for Olivia.

And then Alex took a slip of paper out of his pocket and pushed it across the table toward her. "Here's a check for the rest of the money. I want you to have it now and not after we make love."

His face was unreadable but something softened inside her, despite her pulse leaping all over the place. It was nice to know he was sensitive about her feelings.

"Thank you," she whispered, leaving the check where it was for the moment. She'd paid half of his other generous check into her business account and half into her mother's account in LA. It had held both banks at bay until she could cash this latest check.

As for Alex, any man who put his family first had to have some sort of sensitivity about him, she admitted, liking that he was doing this for his brothers, just as she was doing this partly for her mother. They at least had this in common.

And that reminded her.

She tilted her head at him. "Alex, I like your father. I think his heart's in the right place."

In a split second Alex's jaw hardened. "You've known him five minutes and you figured that out, did you?"

Oh damn. She regretted saying anything now. Their moment of bonding had disappeared.

"Sometimes you don't need to know a person long to know what they're like," she pointed out coolly. "*You* certainly made up your mind about me quickly enough."

A heartbeat passed, then his hard mouth visibly relaxed and the sexy look in his eyes told her seduction was now on his mind. "Yes, I did, didn't I?" Without warning, he reached across and lifted her hand in his, tugging her gently to her feet.

The breath stalled in her throat. Oh heavens. What had she started? "Alex, I—"

"And that's because I know when something feels right," he cut across her, pulling her the few steps toward him around the table, making her tremble, his intention obvious.

"Alex—"

"And you feel right to me, Olivia Valente," he murmured, pulling her onto his lap, his intense gaze holding hers still, just like his warm hand was holding her waist still. "Very, very right."

She licked her lips. "Alex, can we please—"

"Yes, we can," he muttered, and lowered his head.

Four

Alex's mouth covered hers and the room grew silent as he held her, absorbing the texture of her soft skin against his own. He'd only kissed her twice before, so he wanted to stay like this for a while and appreciate every inch of her mouth.

He did for several heartbeats.

But soon he couldn't ignore his need to explore farther. He needed to delve into her luscious mouth, then uncover her bit by bit. He wanted to know the excitement, feel the intensity, learn the mystery of her body.

And he wanted it *now.*

He parted her lips with his own, and her sweet breath slid straight into him. He groaned and took a moment to savor it, before letting his tongue do a silent sweep.

He moved his mouth over hers slowly. And then she started to kiss him back, learning *his* taste, feeling *his* excitement as pleasure surged through him.

When he finally began to ease away, he scraped his teeth lightly across her bottom lip. "Third time's the charm," he murmured, noting the way her pupils had dilated.

She blinked. "Um…third time?"

"This is our third kiss." He bent his head again. "And this…" he needed more "…is our fourth."

He kissed her deeply again before drawing back to place kisses along her smooth jawline. His lips brushed against her earlobe and he lingered there, breathing in the light floral scent of her hair.

After taking his fill, he leaned back and ran a finger along the underside of her chin. Then he followed the column of her throat to where her quickened pulse drummed at its base, down to the first dainty button of her blue robe resting on her cleavage.

His libido climbed.

"Undo it for me," he commanded.

She gasped, her blue eyes widening. "The button?"

"Yes." He only had one hand free, the other was holding her by the waist. "Then undo the rest of them."

Her eyes were hesitant beneath her long eye-lashes, but after a moment she lifted her hands and began to do as he asked. The silk parted as button after button broke free, leaving behind the blue silk gown made to capture a man's attention.

It did.

And there was nothing pure about the thoughts running through his mind. "You dazzle me," he rasped, seeing the outline of two dark nipples peeking through the shiny material.

He felt her quiver as his thumb ran over the tip of one bud. He did it again, then held the nipple between his finger and thumb, squeezing lightly. Her quiver turned to a shudder.

Relishing the feel of her coming alive under his hands, he bent his head to that breast and began sucking through the material, flicking her with his tongue.

She gave a whimper and her head arced back against his shoulder. One of her arms came around his neck and she held on to him, burying her face in his nape and breathing deeply. Just as quickly, she pulled back, as if caught doing something she shouldn't.

He felt heat explode inside him. "Do that again," he muttered against her breast.

She froze for a split second, hesitated before she did it again, making him groan. They stayed like that for a short time, then finally he lifted his head and she moved her face back.

He looked into her eyes. "A man could lose himself in you and never want to be found," he rasped.

Her eyes darkened. "Oh, Alex."

His gaze slowly slid down her body to where the material pooled at the apex of her thighs. He looked up. "You don't like me saying that?"

"Yes." She swallowed. "I do."

His palm slid downward, over her abdomen and her soft mound before resting between her legs. She gasped as he stroked her with his finger through the gown. "You don't like me touching you?" he teased huskily.

"Yes…" her throat convulsed "…I do."

He had to feel her naked body. He had to see all her creamy smooth skin. He pushed to his feet, with her in his arms, and stood her in front of him. Then he eased the silky robe off her shoulders, letting it drop to the floor. The matching nightgown was next and he shuddered when he saw how perfect she was.

Their eyes locked.

"Alex," she murmured, her eyes darkening, her cheeks coloring, though she made no attempt to cover herself.

Lifting her, he carried her to the bed. After laying her down he began stripping off his clothes.

Their eyes locked again before her gaze ran down his body and she gave a soft gasp. He knew if he didn't touch her…didn't taste her…wasn't inside her soon…he'd explode.

He joined her on the bed and this time her mouth parted even before their lips touched. He gave a low sound of approval, and she answered his kiss, her hands coming up to cling to his shoulders. Willingly, he let her pull him closer, until his bare flesh was pressed against her soft skin, savoring the aching anticipation.

Breaking away, he heard her moan as he got to his knees and launched a trail of kisses over every inch of her body, marking her as his own. She was smooth all over, but never more velvety than between her thighs. He parted her with his tongue and loved her until she arched under him, her hands threading through his hair wildly until she trembled, then shook, then was hit by a shockwave that went on and on.

He reveled in her release but when her climax

ebbed, he could wait no longer. He rose up over her and reached for a condom in the bedside drawer. There was no question on his part as to whether he would use one. And she didn't ask.

With precision, he rolled it on himself while she lay watching. He was aware of nothing around them. He was tuned in solely to her.

And she was glorious.

He entered her slowly, sensation heightening as he sank deep into her warmth. Her gasp reverberated around the room and he took a moment to let her get used to him.

And then he began to move, to thrust in and out to the rhythm of their bodies. But, before too long, the rhythm wasn't enough. Nothing was enough.

Until she clenched around him and like a flash of white heat he exploded with pleasure.

Olivia woke to find herself curled up against Alex. Her husband.

Her *temporary* husband, she reminded herself as her eyes flew open, knowing there was nothing temporary about the two of them right now. Her body seemed permanently attached to his, her mind now burned by memories of his lovemaking.

There was no escaping how Alex had made her

feel last night. He'd been considerate, yet his need for her had surprised her. It had been so intense, so breathtaking.

It had taken a certain kind of man to do that, keeping it physical, but allowing her some sort of emotional connection that had nothing to do with love.

Her throat went dry. Why was she thinking about love just because she was in a man's arms? Love belonged to other couples. Love was not part of her agreement with Alex, she reminded herself, as she tried to ease away from him and slide out of bed.

"Don't move," he murmured.

She froze.

He rolled to face her, and for a long moment his slate-gray eyes lingered on her face. "Where do you think you're going?" His voice thickened, the heat of his arousal filling the space between them.

She tried to think. "Er…it's time to get up," she said, then immediately felt her cheeks warm.

His lips quirked with male humor. "Are you asking me or telling me?"

She resisted the urge to tease him back. "Telling you."

He gave her a knowing look. "You were fantastic," he said softly.

She blinked at him, her heart sinking. "I was?"

His gaze dropped to her naked breasts. "It's been a while, hasn't it?" he said in a husky tone.

She didn't answer. She couldn't. His words reminded her of Eric, who'd thought nothing of praising her just to take the suspicion away from his affairs.

"Don't be embarrassed because you don't sleep around," Alex continued, his palm sliding over her hip. "I actually like that you don't."

"Double standards, Alex?"

His hand stilled, his gaze sharpened. "Not at all. I've never been one to sleep around." He must have seen the disbelief in her eyes because he stiffened. "And I definitely won't sleep around on my wife."

An odd thrill raced through her, but she still couldn't let her anxiety go. "Yes, but women must throw themselves at you all the time."

His brows drew together, then understanding dawned. "I'm not like your ex-husband, Olivia. Just because women offer doesn't mean I accept."

Still, she couldn't let it be. "Yes, but you must have accepted sometimes."

Suddenly his eyes hardened. "There's only room in this bed for two people. You and me. Not your ex. Whatever happened between you two shouldn't be brought here."

His words were the mental slap she needed. "Yes, you're right."

He held her gaze for a few heartbeats, then his eyes softened. "Let him go, Olivia. Don't let him spoil what we have."

Her stomach quivered. "I don't know that we have anything."

"You don't?" He gave a throaty chuckle and the sound slithered down her spine like warm silk. "Maybe I need to refresh your memory."

Without giving her a chance to argue he slid her across the sheet and pulled her under him. Their bodies touched and that's all it took for flames to spark between them.

And then he took her higher and higher, out of control, until she went up in smoke, leaving an after-burn that continued to glow long after he'd brought her to fulfillment.

When she next awoke she found herself alone amongst the sheets, all that was left of their night together. Then she moved her legs and winced a little.

All?

No, there was *this* reminder, she thought, thankful Alex wasn't there to see her blush. Her body was so pleasurably sore, so very conscious of their lovemaking. She'd used muscles she hadn't used for years.

Remembering, she threw back the sheet and hurried to the bathroom. If she stayed in bed she'd be thinking about last night, and right now she didn't need that. Alex might have made her forget all about Eric during their lovemaking, and he might have made her forget *herself,* but now it was time to keep moving. Otherwise she could be tempted to lie in bed and wait for Alex to come back and join her.

And if he saw her like this then he'd think he held her in the palm of his hands.

No way.

She'd given him a year of her life. She wasn't giving him her soul, too.

After showering, she went downstairs and found her way to a huge sunroom which ran the full length of one side of the house. A table was set for a late breakfast, but there was still no sign of Alex.

Then Harriet appeared, clicking her tongue. "He's in the study catching up on some paperwork, though what paperwork there is to do on the first day of his honeymoon is beyond me." She showed Olivia her seat then started fussing around the table.

As a businesswoman herself, Olivia knew the paperwork never ended, honeymoon or not. And she was rather grateful that Alex was busy, even if she couldn't say that to the other woman. She was supposed to be a blushing bride, after all.

Oh heck. She *was* a blushing bride. She just wasn't a blushing bride *in love* with her husband.

"That's okay, Harriet. I'm not feeling neglected." She gave a smile. "Not with all the attention I'm getting from you."

Harriet stopped her fussing and smiled at Olivia. "We're so happy that you married Alex. He needs someone of his own."

This was news to Olivia. Alex had family—a father, a mother, two brothers. He must have plenty of friends.

Of his own.

Yes, there *was* a difference, she silently admitted. Apart from her mother she had no one of *her* own. Oh, she'd thought she'd found that special person when she'd married Eric, and for a short while she'd believed it. She sighed. Ignorance was sometimes bliss.

Of course, she wasn't ignorant about this marriage. This time she had gone into it with eyes wide open. This was a marriage of convenience. Their work came first and rightly so.

The housekeeper offered to cook up some eggs but Olivia declined and said that cereal was fine. Harriet nodded and left the room.

For the first time Olivia got to look at her surroundings. The room was decorated in soft yellows, pale greens and creamy whites. A fountain stood in one corner, close to wicker chairs and a sofa—a place to sit and relax. Potted plants and paintings filled the room. The large glass dining table she was sitting at was no doubt where Alex had enjoyed many a meal. The view of the ocean from here was unsurpassed.

Just as she finished eating and was drinking her coffee, Alex appeared. She ignored the fact that his sheer presence took her breath away as he walked straight over to her, cradled her face in his hands and brought his lips down to hers.

What a kiss!

Then he eased away, the look in his eyes filled with complete satisfaction before he walked around the other side of the table and sat down.

"Sorry I'm late," he said casually, as if he hadn't just made her tremble. "I got caught up on a telephone call."

His casualness made her elation disappear. No doubt he was used to women being accommodating—to both his kisses and his work demands.

Couldn't he be a little considerate of her sensibilities? What if she had really been in love with him? His treatment would crush her. It was just as well she was a working woman, and could give as good as she got.

She placed her napkin on the table and stood. "That's okay, Alex. I've got a couple of business calls to make myself." She started to leave the room.

"Olivia?"

She stopped to look at him. "Yes?"

"The study's the fourth door on the right."

Was that a gleam of humor in his eyes? Had his mouth just twitched? She inclined her head. "I'll find it."

Once in the study she sat down at the desk, feeling quite proud of herself. Even if he *had* found her little protest silently amusing, she'd still scored a point.

Then she picked up the telephone, but felt rather silly when she realized she had no one to call. Having cleared the decks at work for the week, and with Lianne insisting she only call under dire circumstances, who else was there to phone?

Her mother.

Felicia wouldn't think it strange for her daughter to call and see how she was. Only, when she called the Valente estate in Sydney, the housekeeper said her mother had gone out for the day with Alex's parents.

Sigh. There was no one else she dared call. She knew a lot of people in the States, but they'd think her mad checking in on the day after her marriage.

"Finished your calls yet?"

She looked up to see Alex standing in the study doorway. For a moment she suspected he was being sarcastic, but then she saw that he was serious.

Okay, so he may well have been amused by her antics when she'd left him in the sunroom, but he hadn't actually been disparaging of her work ethic.

"Yes, I have."

"Then let's go for a walk down to the beach."

All at once she realized he'd changed from trousers and a polo shirt into something much more informal. Her eyes slowly slid down the length of his lean body, now clothed in a white T-shirt and tan-colored board shorts, with leather sandals on his feet. He looked like a sun-worshipping surfer ready to tackle the waves.

"Where's your surfboard?" she quipped, not really meaning to be funny.

He grinned. "It dumped me years ago."

Olivia couldn't help but chuckle even as she gathered her breath. Lord, that grin made him look young and carefree, and she had trouble associating this man with the same CEO she'd married.

Quickly, for something to do, she glanced down at the slacks she was wearing. "Give me five minutes to change into something more casual."

"Like some help?"

Her heart bumped against her ribs. "No, thanks. I've been dressing myself a long time now," she said, walking toward the door, trying to appear nonchalant.

"It was the undressing I was more interested in," he teased, moving aside from the doorway, allowing her to pass him.

She hid a smile, otherwise he might think she was encouraging him to come up to the bedroom and make love to her.

She wasn't.

No, definitely not.

"I'll meet you on the front veranda in five minutes," she heard him say as she headed for the stairs.

"Fine."

Olivia deliberately took ten minutes to change into Bermuda shorts and a sleeveless top. Then she applied sunscreen to her exposed areas, and grabbed her sunglasses from her purse and put them on.

"That was a long five minutes," Alex said, his own sunglasses not hiding his scowl as she pushed open the front screen door and stepped out onto the veranda.

"I didn't know we were clock-watching."

"We're not." He glanced at his Rolex, then grimaced. "Habit." Taking off the watch, he placed it on the table behind him. "Now, let's go get some fresh air." He held out his hand.

For some reason she found herself hesitating.

"Harriet's watching from the window," he drawled.

"She is?" She went to turn around but didn't get a chance to look before he stepped forward and slipped his hand around hers, tugging her down the front steps and through the short grass to the side of the house. Hand in hand they started walking along a dirt path leading to the beach.

He slanted her a mocking smile. "See, we actually look like lovers now."

"Oh, but—"

"What? We're not lovers?" He stopped and faced her. "Then who was that gorgeous woman in my arms last night?" Suddenly his smile disappeared, his dark glasses hiding his eyes but not the huskiness in his voice.

She could feel her cheeks warm. "Maybe she was a dream?"

"Oh yeah," he murmured. "She was that."

Her heart flipped over. "Alex, I—" All at once the ocean breeze picked up and swirled around them like a small whirlwind, snapping her out of the moment. "Um…that breeze is pretty strong," she said quickly, then turned and continued to walk, surprised when he let her drop her hand from his. She half expected he would tug her back around to face him, pull her up close and…

He fell into step beside her, not touching her now. "Yes, that breeze is good for clearing out the cobwebs," was all he said.

She ignored a stab of disappointment, but it was her own fault. She could have chosen to stay where she was and let him kiss her. Yet she knew why she hadn't. Despite them being lovers, she wasn't in love with him. For her to initiate making love with him would be the equivalent of walking down the main street of Sydney naked. She'd feel totally exposed.

Ahead, the path looped over a small sand dune and down to a sun-kissed beach, scattered with couples lying on towels or parents playing in the shallows with their children. An older man jogged along the water's edge. A couple of surfboard riders bobbed out in the sea, their wait for larger waves appearing to be in vain today.

She sighed in appreciation. "It's beautiful."

"Yes."

She kicked off her sandals, enjoying the feel of

soft sand trickling through her toes. "It's been ages since I walked along a beach."

He stepped out of his own sandals. "Then what are we waiting for?" When she went to pick up her sandals, he instructed, "Leave them. We'll get them on our way back."

She blinked in surprise. "But won't someone steal them?"

He gave a dismissive shrug. "If they're that desperate then they're welcome to them."

"Oh." She shrugged. "Well, I guess a man like you doesn't need to worry about the cost of things."

A muscle tightened at the edge of his jaw. "A man like me?"

She hesitated, realizing she'd said the wrong thing. "It's just that I noticed you left your Rolex back on the veranda."

"So?"

No getting around it now. "Admit it, Alex. You were born with a silver spoon in your mouth. You take some things for granted."

"I seem to remember you've got one of those silver spoons, too."

"Yes," she admitted slowly, "but I was raised frugally by my grandmother." And while Olivia wouldn't call herself in the least frugal, she still couldn't be so cavalier about things like leaving expensive watches out in the open, or even sandals on the beach.

A mask came down over his face. "I keep what's important."

Five

Olivia stood and watched Alex turn and walk along the sand. His words had been steely and totally no-nonsense—the tough CEO coming to the fore. The hard-hitting man was such a part of him. A woman would be incredibly lucky to have him love her. To be so fiercely protected by him. And he *would* be fiercely protective. She knew that instinctively.

He turned back to her. "Coming?"

His words jarred her from her thoughts and she fell into step beside him. She didn't want to think about Alex and another woman, so she changed the subject to try to break any tension between them. "Do you come here often?"

A moment crept by before he glanced at her from behind his sunglasses. "I usually make it for Christmas with the family. It's good to get away from the city and the December heat."

She nodded. "Sounds wonderful." Oh, how she remembered those long, hot summer Christmases. Her mother had always come home to spend the holidays with her and Nanna and they'd had a great time as a family. Then Nanna had died and the last few years she and Felicia had spent Christmas in LA, and nothing had been quite the same. She supposed that was all a part of growing older.

"You'll get to find out yourself this year, Olivia. Christmas is only a couple of months away."

His words startled her. "But I usually spend Christmas with my mother."

"We'll invite her here then." It was more an order than a suggestion.

"But—"

"It would look odd if you take off for the States and leave your new husband here during the festive season," he pointed out.

"You could always come to LA," she said, not even sure she wanted him there, though she knew it would seem strange without him. Good Lord, and she'd only been married a day.

"No." His voice was firm, his chin stubborn. "My parents will be here and my two brothers. I won't break family tradition."

Something in his tone roused her curiosity. This man was deeper than she'd first thought. And much more family-oriented than he let on. No wonder his father had been able to blackmail his son into getting married.

Marriage to a man like this would have been a dream come true for her if it had been a real marriage. A permanent marriage. She sighed. It was just as well it wasn't a real marriage because then he'd want a real family with her and—

Suddenly he stopped, put his hand on her arm and spun her toward him. She was in his arms before she knew it, his lips against hers, taking her by surprise with a kiss that made her forget they were on a beach for all to see. All that mattered was his kiss. And the next.

He eventually pulled back, but she was unable to read his eyes. And that was the trouble with sunglasses. They hid his eyes as well as her own.

She cleared her throat. "Um…what was that for?"

"Someone's taking pictures of us. I wanted to give him something worthwhile to report."

Her heart thudded to a stop. "How nice."

"I thought so," he said, not seeming to notice her sarcasm as he picked up her hand in a possessive manner and began walking her along the shore, as though she was his girl and he was showing the world exactly that.

She hid her disappointment. "Are we still being followed?" she asked for something to say, trying to find her mental balance, pretending she didn't care about being used for publicity purposes while on their honeymoon.

Then she winced inwardly. What was the matter with her? Their whole marriage was going to be one big publicity event. Could she really blame Alex for taking advantage of that right now?

"No, I can't see him. Anyway, forget it for now. He's going to take our picture whether we want him to or not."

He was right and after another hundred yards she began to relax again. The sound of the water lapping against the shore and the feel of the breeze skimming her cheeks eased her concerns considerably. How could she not relax? This was a perfect setting; it would help even the most stressed person to unwind.

Just then the sun went behind a frothy white cloud, and for a few seconds the world was darkened then just as quickly thrown back into a shower of sunlight. Wanting to capture the scene in her mind, she stopped and whipped off her sunglasses to better appreciate the brighter sunshine and rich colors.

Her fingers itched. "Ooh, the light and colors are just marvelous. I'll have to bring my sketchbook down here and capture it all in a design."

He took off his own dark glasses, his gaze sweeping the beach in front of them, as if looking at it through her eyes. Then he looked at her. "I'd like to watch you design something."

She blushed with pleasure. "I've had an idea for some time to put an Australian mark on an international design. This may be just what I've been looking for."

"You're quite a talent, aren't you?" he said, his eyes full of admiration.

Her heart skipped a beat but she managed a short chuckle. "I haven't designed it yet."

"I have every confidence it will be a winner."

She quickly placed her sunglasses back on to hide her eyes, not wanting him to see she was almost made shy by his praise. "Thank you," she murmured.

Heavens, she was used to being held in high regard by the rich and powerful. She'd designed clothes for some of the most famous people in the world. Yet this man—her husband—made her self-conscious when he praised her talents?

Crazy.

He put his sunglasses on. "Are you ready to go back? I need to get some more work done, I'm afraid."

She nodded. "Okay, but I think I'll grab a sketch-book and come back down while you're working."

"No."

She blinked at his unmistakable air of command. Was she hearing right? "Pardon?"

"I don't want you coming down here by yourself. You could get harassed and I won't be around to help."

"The media are not out in force, Alex. There's only the one guy who—" Suddenly she caught a movement out of the corner of her eye and she spun toward it. Just as quickly she twisted back toward Alex. "That's not a reporter," she hissed of the photographer a couple of yards away. "He's only a kid."

"He's a teenager and now he's just run off, no doubt looking to sell the photographs to the highest bidder." Alex's mouth flattened. "I meant what I said, Olivia. Don't come down here by yourself."

She lifted her chin. "You're blowing things out of proportion."

"Humor me."

"I'd rather strangle you."

He arched a brow but his lips quirked. "That's a bit drastic, don't you think?"

"Look, I'm not used to sitting around all day doing nothing."

"Then it's about time you did. We have a swimming pool up at the house. Why not laze around it for a couple of hours? And I'll take you into town for dinner tonight."

Her pulse leaped at the thought of dinner with him, despite herself. "I'm not a child to be rewarded for keeping out of your way while you're working." Her chin set stubbornly. "As a matter of fact I still have some work to do of my own," she fibbed. "I wasn't going to work on our honeymoon but…" she paused deliberately "…if you're working then I may as well, too."

He tensed, a muscle starting to tick in his jaw. "Sorry about that. My father has been easing off on the work lately and that's put more pressure on me."

"Oh." Something about his words clutched at her heart. Perhaps it was the rough edge of emotion in his voice that made her soften toward him. "Alex, I understand." She still didn't like being told what to do, but she'd cut him a break this time.

He inclined his head, his mouth not as tight as before, his shoulders not as tense. "Good."

Then he cupped her elbow and they walked back up the beach. Surprisingly their sandals were still where they'd left them, but she didn't look at Alex nor did she say a word as they stepped into them and made their way up to the house.

Once there, he took off for the study, reading through a handful of phone messages, already forgetting that she even existed. Olivia watched him go, a silly sense of loneliness filling her. She was never lonely.

It must be because she felt suddenly tired, she decided, and went up to the bedroom to take a shower to wash off the sand.

When she came out, dressed in her silk bathrobe, the bed looked so very inviting. Perhaps if she lay down for just a few minutes….

She woke to find herself covered with a light blanket, the bedside clock showing midafternoon. Feeling guilty, she threw back the blanket, got dressed in white capri pants and a cherry-red top and hurried downstairs. Alex was still in the study, but he put his pen down when he saw her in the doorway.

"I'm sorry," she said. "I didn't mean to fall asleep for so long. It was supposed to be a quick nap."

"No need to apologize. You must have needed it." His gaze traveled down her body, his eyes darkening at every lowering inch. "I was tempted to join you," he murmured, his raspy voice sending a frisson of excitement racing through her.

She moistened her lips. "I thought Harriet might have covered me up."

She hoped.

She prayed.

A faint smile curved the edges of his mouth. "No, it was me."

She gave an inner gasp. Her bathrobe would have covered her, but the fabric was thin….

"By the way, Olivia, you don't snore," he said, his voice silky smooth.

She felt the flush of heat enter her cheeks. "That's good to know." It was time to get out of here. "Um, I missed lunch so I might go get a snack." She half expected he'd want to join her.

But his eyes turned businesslike. "Don't forget I'm taking you to dinner in town. Let's make it seven."

"I'll be ready."

He nodded and picked up his pen. "You'd better go get something to eat."

Before she'd even stepped away to head toward the kitchen, Olivia heard the preoccupation in his voice and knew it wasn't with *her*.

She sighed as that strange sense of loneliness filled her again, but she quickly pushed it aside. She had too much time on her hands right now, that's all. It wasn't that she was feeling like a neglected bride.

Not at all.

Alex sat back in his chair after Olivia left and tried to focus on his work again, but she unsettled him and he wasn't sure he liked being unsettled. Never before had he ever let a woman distract him from his work. He was usually able to keep the two things separate. He liked it that way.

Of course, he'd never been married before.

Never had a woman living with him.

Never had a woman on his family turf.

The family's Christmases had always been here at Villa Valente with his parents and his two brothers and sometimes various relatives, but neither he nor his brothers had brought their girlfriends here. None of them would ever give a woman that false sense of power over them.

Yet having Olivia here now wasn't about giving her the wrong impression. Olivia already knew the score. This year they would be together, and next year they wouldn't be, and that was the way they both liked it.

And the way they both wanted it.

It had to be that way.

For now he'd enjoy the benefits of having a beautiful woman in his life—and in his bed. Making love to Olivia last night for the first time had been amazing. She'd been married before so he hadn't expected to be her teacher, yet there had been an innocence about her, as though he was the first lover to give her more than he took.

And in the giving he'd been given back far more than he'd ever expected. She'd turned into a more than willing pupil. He hadn't been joking when he'd said she'd been a dream to make love to.

And this afternoon when she'd been sleeping…if he hadn't known she was so exhausted he'd have woken her up with a kiss to that gorgeous mouth of hers. And then he'd have kissed her all over before making her his again.

Hell, just thinking about it sent the blood pounding to his groin but he told himself that waiting would make it all the sweeter. Later this evening he would wine and dine her, then make love to her over and over.

But that was easier said than done when he saw her later coming down the stairs dressed in a short brandy-colored dress that showed off her gorgeous curves and long slim legs. Its off-the-shoulder design highlighted a tanned collarbone that deserved to be kissed.

She was exquisite.

He wished now that he'd stayed in their bedroom and watched her dress, smoothing silk stockings up along her legs. Of course if he'd stayed they'd still be in the bedroom.

In bed.

And he'd be inside her.

"I'm going to make love to you later," he said huskily as she approached him. "You know that, don't you?"

A becoming flush stained her cheeks. "So you're not sick of me yet?" she joked.

He frowned. Where had that come from? Her ex?

"No way, sweetheart," he growled, then put his hand under her chin and gave her a hard kiss, more than satisfied by the hint of pleasure he saw in her eyes when he pulled back. "Come on. Let's get out of here." He cupped her elbow and led her out to one of his father's Mercedes. If they didn't go to dinner soon, they'd never get there.

Fifteen minutes later, they were sitting in an intimate corner of the best restaurant in town and Alex was studying the blond beauty in front of him. He could have been sitting amongst the Miss World contestants and none of them would hold a candle to Olivia.

Her eyelids flickered. "Stop staring, Alex," she said in a throaty voice.

"Why?"

She shot him a wry look. "Okay, let's change the subject. Tell me about your Italian background."

"Why?"

Her gorgeous lips curved upward. "Because I've just realized I've never asked you before. I mean, I know what I've read in the papers and that you're Australian-born, but that's about all I know about you."

He leaned back in his chair, pleased she was interested enough to ask. "What do you want to know?"

"Can you speak Italian, for one thing? You never do."

"My grandparents came out from Italy after the war and they taught me when I was growing up, but I prefer to speak Australian." He'd loved his grandparents but they were gone now and he had no interest in speaking Italian with his father.

"And your father?" she said, honing in like a dentist's drill on a sore tooth. "He speaks fluent Italian, doesn't he? Was he born in Italy?"

Alex's brows drew together. "I thought this was about me, not my father."

She cooled a little. "I'm only trying to understand the man I married."

"Don't," he snapped, then grimaced at the withdrawal on her face. He sighed. "Look, my father was twelve when he came here. Eventually he made his millions and later married my mother when he was around thirty. She was Australian and she died when I was little. That's it."

Her eyes softened and filled with sympathy. "I'm sorry."

His stomach knotted. "Yeah, so am I."

The only vague memory he had of his mother was of sitting on her knee. He also had a couple of old photographs. She'd been raised by an elderly aunt so he hadn't even been able to ask her family about her. Cesare Valente certainly hadn't wanted to talk about her.

The only reason he'd known why he was called Alexander and not the Italian form, Alessandro, was because Isabel had told him his own mother had insisted on it. Surprisingly, Cesare had kept that pattern when Nick and Matt were born. In some corner of Alex's heart, he liked to think his father had done it out of respect for his first wife. On the other hand, perhaps that was just foolish thinking.

"What about your grandparents, Alex?" Olivia asked, drawing him from his thoughts. "They're not still alive, are they? I didn't see them at the wedding, but no one has mentioned them."

"They died years ago after a long and happy

marriage." He gave a harsh laugh. "I can't say the same for my father," he said, thinking about his father's three marriages.

She tilted her head. "But Cesare has been married to Isabel for a long time now. They seem very happy."

He scowled. "They are," he grudgingly admitted. "I guess I have to give him credit for that."

She nodded. "It's probably part of the reason he wanted to see you married." Then she hesitated, as if she wasn't sure whether to say something or not. "He cares for you, Alex. You may not be able to see it, but I can."

"Perhaps." He wondered what she'd think if he told her his father wanted him to have an heir, too. But why mention something that wasn't necessary? In six months time Cesare would be on his way to retirement, if not before. He wouldn't be able to dictate to any of his sons after that.

The arrival of the waiter to deliver their drinks gave Alex the chance to end the discussion, but as he watched Olivia smile her thanks at the young man, he felt a jolt inside his chest. If he had to have someone have his child, she would be the perfect choice.

He pushed that thought aside. "Now it's your turn. Tell me about your ex-husband," he said, watching her stiffen. He knew what the papers had said about the other man, but he wanted to hear Olivia's version of it all.

She held his gaze. "I met Eric when I was just starting out as a designer. I was working in Paris and he was this really handsome, debonair Englishman. I'd never met anyone like him before." A derisive sound emerged from her throat. "I don't want to meet anyone like him again."

"He cheated on you." It was a statement, not a question.

Her expression clouded. "Yes. He thought I had a personal fortune because of my mother. When he discovered that she wasn't supporting me as much as he thought, he dumped me for a woman who had more money."

Anger rippled through Alex. "The bastard."

She inclined her head. "Thanks. I know it sounds horrible, but by that stage I was glad to get rid of him."

"No, what sounds horrible is him using you the way he did."

"Thank you," she whispered. She looked hesitant, then said, "He's the main reason I have trouble trusting people these days."

Alex knew that took a lot to admit. "Yet, as a stranger, you trusted me enough to marry me."

Her tight expression relaxed into a smile. "Yeah, go figure."

Something warmed inside him, but before he could savor the moment, their meal arrived. The food was superb and afterward they strolled along the promenade. He couldn't wait to get her home and make love to her.

And when they finally made it to their bedroom and he pulled her into his arms, he felt her tremble from head to toe in a way that none of his other lovers ever had. It made him feel special, as though he was the only man on earth who could fulfill her needs.

And that affected him more than anything.

Six

The next morning, Olivia couldn't settle. She and Alex rose late then had breakfast together in the sunroom, but he was preoccupied and soon afterwards went to the study to work. She knew he had a lot to prepare with the launch of the perfume in a few weeks' time, but she still had to fight that feeling of neglect again. So she made calls to Lianne and her mother, only to find they were still getting along just fine without her.

Everyone seemed to be busy except her.

She needed to throw herself into work.

Without warning a vision came to her for her next

design and she remembered the colors of the light-blue sky blending with the dark-blue ocean spilling white froth along the golden sand. The effect was eye-catching and perfect for her next designs.

She would call it the Valente Collection, she decided. After all, she was a Valente now, if only temporarily. And Alex had said they could eventually combine her designs with Valente's Woman perfume.

She hurried to find her sketchbook and pencils, intending to sit on the balcony and draw with the full view of the ocean before her. Only, this far away the vibe wasn't quite the same. She needed to get up closer and steep herself in the colors and textures of the scene. It was important that she connect with her surroundings.

Alex need never know, she decided as she left the house. Heck, she wasn't going to be told what to do anyway. If she wanted to go down to the beach, she would. This was her work, and she wasn't going to miss out on an opportunity just to appease a husband who was busy with his own work anyway.

Of course, walking along the dirt path to the beach hadn't seemed scary when she was with Alex, but now she could hear all sorts of noises in the grass that reminded her of snakes.

She picked up a long stick just in case, and made sure her footsteps trod heavily, hoping any slithery surprises would hear her coming and disappear into the longer grass.

It was a relief when she reached the beach, but she didn't want to think about the walk back to the house so she put it out of her mind. In next to no time, she'd made herself comfortable on the sand, with a small grassy dune at her back as she reached for her pencils, blocked out the world and began to let the magic take over.

She had no idea how long she stayed there, but it wasn't until a shadow fell across her that she realized it must have been a while, perhaps even a couple of hours. She looked up and angled her chin, expecting it to be Alex. Only the man standing there didn't resemble her husband at all.

In his fifties, he leaned forward and looked at the design on the paper. "Is that going to be in your next collection?"

A reporter.

Ignoring him, she quickly closed her sketchbook and got to her feet. In her haste, she dropped the book and gasped when he scooped it up before she could.

She held out her hand. "That belongs to me. If you don't return it I'll call the police."

"Little lady, I intend to return it," he said with a smirk. "After you answer a few questions for me."

An interview.

"Look, you obviously know who I am. You must also know that I'm on my honeymoon." She wanted to snatch the book out of his hand, but she made herself stay calm.

"Speaking of honeymoons, I'm surprised your husband lets you out of his sight."

She knew that whatever she said could be miscon- strued. If she said Alex was working, this man would make something of it and report that their marriage was already on the rocks. If she said Alex was napping, the papers would report him ill, or worse, on his deathbed.

"He'll be along shortly," she said, hoping to give herself time to reason with this man.

He snorted.

And then, miracle of miracles, she saw Alex striding toward them, a thunderous expression on his face that she knew was for her. "See, I told you," she told the older man and was pleased to see him blanch. Good. He was nothing but a bully.

"What's going on here?" Alex demanded, step- ping close, putting himself between her and the other man in a protective fashion.

She could afford to relax a little now. "Alex, no need to worry. I dropped my sketchbook and this, er…man was just giving it back." She held out her hand. "I'll take that now, thank you."

The reporter looked at Alex then at her, then finally gave it back. "Here we are, little lady."

Olivia took it, pretending she didn't want to snatch it to her breast. And if he called her "little lady" again she'd probably hit him with it.

Alex turned to Olivia. "Right. Lunch is ready," he said, then taking her by the elbow he shot the other man a hard look and led her away, a bit like a hardened criminal on the run. Any moment now, she expected him to bring out the handcuffs.

Once out of earshot and on the dirt path back to the house, he growled, "What the hell were you thinking, coming down here by yourself?"

She shrugged, hoping to dislodge his hand, but his grip was firm. "I needed to do my designs and the best place for that was down here at the beach."

"I told you I would bring you down here myself."

"You were working. I didn't want to disturb you."

"I *prefer* that you disturb me." He shot her a searing sideways gaze. "See what can happen when you don't listen?"

She frowned. "Don't you think you're overreacting a little?"

His jaw clenched. "No."

"But—"

"No buts. The guy was a reporter who would have stolen your designs if I hadn't turned up. And there wouldn't have been a bloody thing you could have done about it."

"I'd have charged him with theft," she said with more bravado than she felt.

He flashed her a look of disdain. "So you know his name then? You know where he lives? And you have proof he stole your designs?"

She grimaced. Put like that…

"It's as well you came along then," she conceded, glad to see they were coming up to the house. Anger radiated from him in waves, and this would be a good time to escape to the bedroom.

Without warning he halted, a pulse beating in his cheekbone. "You just don't get it, do you? You don't know what could have happened. You don't know—" He stopped, let go of her elbow before he expelled a breath, then stormed off with a snarled, "Forget it."

She stared after him in surprise, his back ramrod straight as he strode past the front steps and down the side of the house to the rear. What on earth was his problem? This was definitely over the top.

Then she realized Harriet was standing on the

veranda watering some potted plants, her face full of concern.

Olivia let out a slow breath and continued walking to the house, then up the steps. She wasn't sure how much she should say, if anything, but Harriet was no fool.

"He found you then?" the older woman said, putting the small watering can down on the table.

Olivia nodded. "Yes."

Harriet sighed. "He was concerned when he couldn't find you. He seemed to know you'd gone down to the beach."

Olivia gave a defensive shrug, still stinging from Alex's reaction. "I decided to do some drawings, that's all. I'm not sure why that's a problem."

The other woman's eyes softened. "Olivia, don't be too hard on him. He has his reasons for getting upset. *All* the Valente men do."

Olivia's forehead creased. "Why? What do you mean?"

"His mother, Isabel, was attacked on that beach twenty years ago," Harriet said, making Olivia gasp. "It was late afternoon and they'd all gone down there for a swim. Afterward they were coming back here when Isabel realized she'd left a beach towel behind and she went back to get it." She winced. "No one thought anything of it."

"And?"

"For some reason, Alex decided to go back and check on her while the others continued walking home. When he got there, the beach was deserted except for some drunk who was trying to force her to the ground. Alex was only fifteen but he got the man away from her. Then Nick appeared and the police were called and the man was charged with assault, but everyone was horrified at what could have happened."

"Oh my God," Olivia murmured, picturing it all. No wonder Alex had been adamant she not go down there alone. To find his stepmother being attacked must have been terrible.

"No one ever talks about it," Harriet continued, "but it's always at the back of our minds. Alex would have been worried something might happen to you."

Olivia shivered in the heat of the day. "Thank you for telling me, Harriet. At least I understand now."

"And that's half the battle," Harriet said, smiling in sympathy.

Olivia gave a small smile in return. "Yes."

But she had to wonder what the other half of the battle would be.

Olivia stayed out of Alex's way for the rest of the day, while he stayed in the study working. She felt bad now for giving him such a fright. If only he'd told her what had happened with Isabel at the beach, she'd have understood and tried not to worry him.

Poor Isabel. It must have been a terrible experience for her.

And poor Alex. He'd be the first to save anyone from being hurt, not just a loved one.

Not that *she* was a loved one. Not in that sense. No, being Alex's wife didn't mean anything more than that he would protect her if she needed it.

So why did she feel strangely disappointed it wasn't more than that?

Pushing that thought aside, and as a peace offering, she decided to have a candlelit dinner for the two of them. She put her head together with Harriet and they came up with a rack of lamb with roast pumpkin salad, followed by a berry ice cream log.

Then Olivia lazed by the pool for the rest of the afternoon, working on her designs until just before six. She was glad that Alex didn't seek her out, and suspected he was still in the study.

He was.

He put down his pen and leaned back in the leather chair, when she entered the room. She told him Harriet was preparing a special dinner for them.

"What time?" he said, distractedly.

"Seven-thirty."

He looked at his watch, then back at her. "I'll be there."

She frowned. "You shouldn't be working so hard, Alex."

A shadow of irritation crossed his face. "It has to be done."

"Harriet won't forgive you if you fall asleep in her dinner."

He held her eyes for a moment, then straightened and picked up his pen. "I'll be fine."

She paused. "You won't forget, will you?"

"I'll be there," he said without looking up.

Aware she was being dismissed, she went up to the bedroom and took her time dressing in one of her own designs that was casual yet dressy enough for dinner. She was just putting the finishing touches to her makeup when she heard the splash of someone diving into the swimming pool outside.

Going to the side window, she looked down and saw Alex doing laps of the pool. He was magnificent as he sliced through the water, his broad shoulders tanned and toned, no doubt getting rid of pent-up energy.

And that was a good thing, she thought, tempted to stay and watch some more, but forcing herself to go down to the kitchen to check that everything was set with Harriet.

She was in the dining room, unnecessarily straightening the settings on the table, when Alex came into the room right on seven-thirty. Dressed in beige cargo pants and a blue shirt, he looked fresh and vital and more handsome than ten men put together.

His gaze slid over her white sleeveless dress flaring gently to her calves, a gold belt looping her waist. A glint of approval in his eyes made her stomach dip before he transferred his gaze to the flickering candelabra.

There was a slight lift of his brow. "Candles? It's not even dark yet."

She ignored his lack of romanticism. "I know, but it adds a nice touch, don't you think?" She gestured with her hand. "Here. Sit down. The food's all ready to be served from this trolley here." It had hot and cold compartments.

"Harriet isn't serving us?" he asked, coming forward and holding out a chair for her first, then sitting opposite her.

"No. She and Martin have gone into town to watch a movie."

His lips twisted as he looked over the table. "At least we've convinced Harriet this is a real marriage."

She blinked. "This wasn't Harriet's idea. It was mine."

His glance sharpened. "I see."

She squared her shoulders. "I wanted to apologize, Alex. For this morning. I didn't know about Isabel being attacked."

His eyes shuttered even more than usual. "I see Harriet's been talking too much."

She tilted her head. "That's why you didn't care about leaving the sandals on the beach. It reminds you of Isabel going back for the towel, doesn't it?"

The line of his mouth tightened and his shoulders stiffened, but a second later he reached over and lifted the wine bottle out of the ice bucket. "I don't like to analyze things," he said in a nonchalant fashion that didn't fool her one bit.

No, he wouldn't, she thought, watching him as he poured her a glass of wine, then one for himself. "I'm surprised your father didn't sell up after that."

A muscle jerked in his jaw. "No, we love it here," he said brusquely.

She nodded. This would be the one place they must all feel like a family, despite him not getting on with his father over the years. And for that reason it must be very special to Alex.

She took a sip of wine before saying, "Why didn't

you explain it to me? I would have understood. I wouldn't have gone down there alone if I'd known."

His gaze speared hers. "You trusted me enough to marry me, but perhaps you've got to learn to trust me in other ways."

She winced, his remark taking the wind out of her sails. Placing her trust in someone wasn't exactly the easiest thing for her to do. It was the hardest. She knew he understood where she was coming from but—

"Yes, I suppose that's the next step," she quietly agreed.

Just then the evening sun shone through the windows of the sunroom and caught the angles of Alex's face, throwing part of it in shadow.

She realized something then. For all his talk about trust, he was the one keeping something of himself in the shadows. *He* hadn't explained why he hadn't told her about Isabel in the first place.

Trust worked both ways, didn't it?

She opened her mouth to say all this to him, but another thought hit her. Or was this about something rather than trust? Was this more about him not sharing his emotions with her? His fears?

Yes, it was.

And as much as she hated to admit it, Alex's attitude was a refreshing change when all the men in her life—her stepfathers, even Eric to a deceptive degree—had been the first to share their fears with her.

Everything, actually.

They'd nearly driven her mad with their confidences. If she had to choose, she'd prefer a man who didn't need to share too many of his feelings. There was a time and a place for talking but she definitely liked the strong, silent type.

Alex was one of those.

Something softened inside her. "Alex, do you think our dinner will spoil if we leave it for a while?"

He scowled. "I shouldn't think so. Why?"

She got to her feet and held out her hand. "I want to make love to you, Alex," she said huskily. "Do you mind?"

He looked shocked but recovered quickly. "I'd be a fool if I did." He got to his feet and put his hand in hers. "And I'm no fool."

Seven

At the end of the week they returned to Sydney and moved straight into Alex's luxurious apartment at Woolloomooloo, with its spectacular city, park and harbor views and just a short stroll from the center of the city itself.

Now that Alex was back at work and she had a lot of time to herself, Olivia banked the other check that he'd given her the night of their wedding.

Her mother had excitedly returned to the States on the Valentes' private jet, having been called back for a second audition in the movie she'd been coveting. Olivia prayed her mother would win the part.

As for herself, she was excited about the designs she'd created while at Villa Valente, and during the following week she settled into working on them at her Sydney boutique while helping Lianne arrange a fashion show soon to be held in Melbourne.

And then, one evening the following week, Alex said during dinner, "We'll be going to the States on Friday."

Olivia's fork of salmon stopped in midair. "We're going in two days?"

He nodded. "The launch is set for the twentieth, but they need us there a couple of days earlier for some other publicity."

She took a deep breath and placed her fork back down on her plate. "You didn't tell me it was going to be so soon."

"You didn't ask."

"But that's the day of my fashion show in Melbourne. Lianne arranged it months ago. I have to be there."

His eyes hardened. "No. You *have* to be at the perfume launch with me. Let Lianne handle the fashion show by herself. She has staff to help her."

She didn't like the way he was dismissing her

commitments. "It's *my* name on the collection and it's *my* show, Alex. I need to be there. Lianne's gone to a lot of trouble to get this all up and running."

"And I've gone to a lot of trouble to get the launch up and running," he said, totally uncompromising.

"But I need all the business I can get." She'd paid off most of her debts but there were still ongoing ones, not the least her mother if she didn't get that part in the movie.

"Olivia, you made a deal with me."

He was right but still, his arrogance was showing again. "So this is what the next year is going to be like, is it? I'm to drop everything to fit in with your plans?"

"Yes." There was no hesitation.

She shot him a withering look. "I'm not some housewife from the fifties, you know. I have a job outside the home. I have responsibilities to others."

"No, you have a responsibility to me. It was the reason I married you, remember?" he said with cutting emphasis. "If you renege on the deal then it's all been for nothing."

Hearing him say it like that made her feel less than worthless. She had been a commodity, that's all. After the past two weeks she'd thought their lovemaking had brought them closer together. She'd thought that their getting to know each other a little might have counted.

Obviously it hadn't.

Her throat tightened. "I'll see what I can do."

"Good." His eyes said he expected it all to be sorted to his satisfaction, and no doubt every woman he had ever known had done exactly that. How she wished her hands weren't tied over this.

When Olivia went to the boutique the next morning and told Lianne of her dilemma, the other woman was as dismayed as she was about the situation, but then she became philosophical about it all. Knowing that her partner was able to handle the upcoming show without her made Olivia feel better.

Amazingly, in late afternoon, Lianne came into Olivia's office to tell her the venue for the show had been cancelled.

"You don't think—" Lianne began, then stopped.

"What?"

She shrugged. "No, nothing."

Olivia had a suspicious gnawing in her stomach. "Do you think Alex arranged this?"

Lianne looked uncomfortable. "It occurred to me just for a moment, Olivia, but Alex is an aboveboard kind of guy," she rushed to assure her. "He wouldn't do anything underhanded."

Olivia wasn't so sure, but she couldn't say that. She wanted no one to know that she didn't have complete faith in her husband.

"No, he wouldn't do anything underhanded," she agreed, despair ripping at her insides.

She'd already been through one husband who had cheated on her, so that she had married another man who cheated her in another way was easier to believe. And if she didn't believe that, what other explanation could there be for the cancellation? No, it was too much of a coincidence.

By the time she arrived home she had worked herself into a bit of a tizz. It was bad enough that *she* suspected Alex of manipulating the situation, but knowing that Lianne suspected it as well embarrassed and humiliated her.

She found him shaving at the bathroom sink, a towel around his lean hips, his broad back tanned, muscular and crying out for a woman's touch.

Pain instantly twisted inside her. Oh God, shades of Eric?

"Going out somewhere, Alex?" she snapped.

He didn't appear surprised by her presence, so must have heard her coming through the apartment. "I have a business dinner to attend," he said, smoothing the razor along his jawline. "At the Teppanyaki."

She remembered now. A few days ago he'd told her about the invitation for the men-only dinner with a Japanese billionaire.

Fine. So he wasn't meeting another woman. One thing had nothing to do with the other anyway, she thought, swallowing a silly sense of relief that he wasn't seeing someone else.

She stepped into the large marble bathroom and went up to him. "You got them to cancel the venue, didn't you?"

He looked blank. "I don't know what you mean."

"The venue for my fashion show in Melbourne has fallen through. They said there's a problem with the wiring. How convenient," she sneered.

His blank look disappeared and his mouth clamped into a thin line beneath the remaining shaving cream. "And you think I arranged it?"

"Yes."

For a moment everything went still. Something hard flared in his eyes, then cleared, and just as quickly he turned back to the sink, obviously ignoring her. Without thinking, she reached out to stop him, but instead her hand slipped along his damp skin and accidentally knocked the towel away.

Time stopped.

Even her gasp seemed to be made in slow motion.

Then she felt drawn to look downward. He was fully aroused. Heat washed over her and slowly she raised her gaze to his.

His eyes held an odd glitter. "Touch me," he rasped.

She hesitated, unable to move.

"Touch me," he repeated.

The command excited her, and she moistened her lips, seeing him tense at the action. Suddenly she wanted to see how much further she could arouse him.

Almost in a trance she reached out…and slowly…deliciously…wrapped her palm around him, gripping him fully. He felt so smooth, so firm, so incredibly male. A woman could do much to torment a man like this.

Her fingertips moved to do just that.

Instantly he put his hand over hers, stilling her. Anticipation leaped inside her, making her wonder what he would—

"You trust my body, Olivia," he muttered. "So why can you still not trust *me?*"

His words were like a slap in the face. She swallowed hard and tried to pull her thoughts together. She dropped her hand away from him. "I—"

"Think about it," he said coolly, and turned back to the sink to complete his shave, not bothering to cover himself with the towel on the floor.

For a moment more she stood there, warring emotions running through her. Then she spun away, needing time to be alone.

"Olivia?"

She stopped but didn't look back.

"We'll finish this later tonight."

She didn't reply, her heart jumping in her throat. What exactly did he want to finish? Their discussion?

Or their marriage?

Olivia was in the kitchen making a cup of coffee when she heard the apartment door close. Her chest ached with a growing pain. Alex had left without saying goodbye.

Well, she wouldn't let thinking about Alex overwhelm her. She would have dinner, do some paperwork, then go to bed, just as she did every night.

Only, the massive bed seemed so empty without Alex. She tossed and turned, remembering the scene in the bathroom, her heart skipping a beat at how blatantly aroused he'd been for her.

And then her heart sank just as quickly when she remembered how fast he'd turned away. Angry, she got out of bed and made for the spare bedroom, where she tossed and turned some more. She must have fallen asleep eventually, for she awoke as the bedside lamp was turned on.

She groaned and pulled the blanket up over her head. "Turn the light off, Alex."

He didn't answer.

Suddenly the blankets were thrown back and she was being scooped up in his arms. Her eyes flew open. "Alex?"

A pulse leaped along the hard line of his jaw. "You're my wife. You sleep beside me."

A thrill zipped through her, but she lifted her chin in the air. "I'm only a temporary wife, Alex."

"Then you'll sleep with me temporarily." He walked into their bedroom, placed her on the bed and stood looking over her. "Now, do you really believe that I cancelled the venue?"

Her gaze became trapped in his, and realization clutched at her heart. His stance was defiantly male, trying to show her he didn't care if she didn't trust him.

But she suddenly knew beyond doubt that he did care.

And she suddenly knew he'd had nothing to do with the venue cancellation for the fashion show. She'd just been letting her fears and prejudices get the better of her.

"No, Alex," she whispered. "I don't believe you did that at all now."

His expression shifted with the barest hint of relief, but his shoulders gave him away. The tension seemed to ease out of him before he turned the light out and she heard him shedding his clothes.

Then the bed moved as he slid into it and pulled her up close against his chest. "Now, where were we…" he said, his voice thickening.

The next day they headed to the States in the Valentes' private jet. Alex had a heavy schedule on arrival in Los Angeles so he had to get some paperwork out of the way first. Eventually he was able to sit back, relax and enjoy the breather.

And enjoy the beautiful woman opposite him in the lounge area of the aircraft.

Even when she made him mad.

For a while there last evening, he'd been so angry with her he'd barely been able to eat dinner. How the hell could she think he'd had something to do with the cancellation of the venue? He'd never do something like that.

Okay, he'd been determined she would accompany him to the States today, but everything he did was direct and upfront. No deceitfulness for him, and especially not when it came to family.

And right now, Olivia was family.

His immediate family.

His.

Watching her, something began to unfurl deep inside him. It just seemed so damn right having her here with him. All at once he wasn't so sure he wanted to let her go when the year was up.

And if that were the case, would she be amenable to staying? Perhaps to stretching it out for a few more years after that? Perhaps he could even fulfill *all* of his father's ultimatum?

It was crazy, but he now felt an odd lump in his throat at the thought of being a father. It was something he'd never cared about before, but with Olivia here beside him it didn't seem so unimportant.

They were halfway over the Pacific Ocean when he said, "How would you feel about having my child?"

Her head snapped up from reading a book. "Wh-what?"

If it hadn't been so serious he would have felt amused at her reaction. "I'd like to father a child and I'd like to have that child with you, Olivia. Do you have any objections?"

She was still gaping in shock. Her mouth opened and closed, then she swallowed hard. "Plenty," she croaked.

His brows drew together. "I think we'd make good parents."

She took a deep breath. "I have no doubt about that, Alex, but that's not the problem."

"Then what is?"

Her expression clouded as she placed her book on the coffee table between them. "You never said anything about children before."

A cold knot began to form in his stomach. "I know, but I've been thinking—"

"Don't." She winced. "I mean, why would you ask me this now? It's so out of the blue."

Hell. He suddenly didn't want her thinking he had growing feelings for her. Her reaction was enough to know they wouldn't be welcome. Not at all. He had to make her believe this was all about his father.

"Olivia, I didn't tell you everything about my father's ultimatum. There was more he wanted than just that I get married." He let a moment slide by. "My wife has to conceive an heir within twelve months or I still risk losing the inheritance."

The blood drained from her face. "Oh God."

Apprehension rolled through Alex at her reaction. He wasn't sure why.

She drew a breath. "Why didn't you tell me about this before?"

"Ours was…is…" he emphasized, "only a temporary marriage. I didn't see it as an issue at the time."

She frowned. "I don't understand, Alex. What's changed?"

The plane started to bounce around as they hit a patch of turbulence and Alex was grateful for the distraction.

"I've decided I'd like to stay married to you for a few more years. And if we could produce a child in that time, even better."

She sucked in a sharp breath. "No," she murmured, looking horrified.

Mixed feelings surged through him. On the one hand he understood her being taken by surprise, on the other, was it so horrible that he wanted his wife to have his child?

"I thought if we both felt the same way," he began. "We could—"

"This is so not fair, Alex," she cut across him.

"But—"

"No, I'm sorry." A look of resolve grew in her eyes. "I can't help you with this."

Anger sparked inside him. She hadn't even given it any thought. "Can't or won't?"

Before she could answer, the plane bounced even more roughly and he saw the flare of fear in her eyes. He suddenly didn't feel too at ease himself.

All at once the moment was more important than their future. "Make sure you're strapped in," he warned as he reached for the phone flashing a red light beside him.

"You, too," she murmured, a look in her eyes that said she was just as worried about him as for herself. And that made him realize that she cared about him.

How much, he wasn't sure.

As much as she was scared about the turbulence, Olivia was thankful for the interruption. Being bounced around inside an aircraft and fearing for her life was a good companion to the turmoil inside her. How could Alex have thrown her for a loop like this? Why would he want her to have his child?

The child she could never have.

Dear Lord, this was one of the reasons she had agreed to a temporary marriage in the first place. She'd thought she had no need to worry about giving Alex children and that he need never know that she really *was* less than perfect.

Her heart squeezed at the thought of her baby, lost to an ectopic pregnancy. And at the loss of any future babies she should've had. Oh, how she wished she was capable of having a baby.

Alex's baby.

Yet how could she tell him? She had to. And she would, once they were back on terra firma and in the privacy of their hotel suite with time to talk properly.

Only, after they landed—the turbulence having finally ended—they were surprised by an invitation to a luncheon with one of the most powerful men in California. It was impossible to refuse, despite being jetlagged, so they quickly dressed at their hotel and then were whisked away to his mansion in Bel-Air.

So it was early evening before they returned to their hotel suite. Olivia wanted to get what she had to say out of the way, but decided a while longer wouldn't matter. They both needed to shower and have a light dinner and unwind before she dropped her bombshell.

Unwind?

Yeah, right.

That wasn't possible, she decided as she went to return a call from her mother while Alex showered and changed.

Felicia was excited about having been offered a part in a television series, so she didn't notice that her daughter wasn't quite herself. Her mother now had the dilemma of whether to accept the part or wait to hear if she would get the role in the movie, and she asked Olivia to convey her regrets to Alex that she

now wasn't able to come to the perfume launch in
New York as she'd planned.

"I didn't know she *was* coming," Olivia said to Alex
over dinner, after she told him the rest of her mother's
news. As a fashion designer she'd thought *she* would
be enough, along with the Cannington name of course.
It wasn't that she minded, but she did mind Alex not
telling her he'd invited her mother in the first place.

Alex shrugged. "She mentioned it at our wedding,
but I thought no more of it."

She frowned, accepting what he said but more
interested in his attitude to her at this very moment.
He'd played the perfect husband this afternoon when
they'd been in the company of others, but now, in
private, he was withdrawn and cool.

"Why not?" she said to be contrary. "My mother
would have been a good asset to have there with us."

"Frankly, I like Felicia but she's not the type in
whose promises I would put any store." There was a
tiny pause. "Not like you."

She should take offence at what he'd said about
her mother but she was more concerned with what
he was implying about *her.*

Her chin angled. "I didn't promise to have your
baby, Alex."

A muscle tensed at the edge of his jaw. "I know."

"So don't accuse me of something I haven't done."

For a moment he looked as if he would argue, then remorse flashed across his face and he expelled a deep breath. "Yes, you're right. You made no such promise." He pushed back his chair and stood.

She reached out and put her hand over his. "Alex, please don't go. I mean, we really do need to talk about…" she hesitated "…about what you mentioned on the plane."

He stilled, then gave a jerky nod of his head and sat back in his chair. "Go ahead."

Her stomach was churning, but she had to proceed. "Alex, I need to say this. I have to make it clear to you that…" She swallowed. "*Why* I can't have your child."

"So you don't like children then? Is that the problem?"

"I love children," she said in a ragged whisper, pain and despair wrapping around her heart. "Alex, I want children more than anything and if I could, I would love to have your child."

A lump rose in her throat. She had to say it, had to put an end to his hopes. "Only I…can't. I'm infertile. I've been told I'll never have a child."

Eight

Alex felt the bottom fall out of his world. Up until this moment he had had no doubt Olivia would come around and have his baby.

She was staring at him with pain-filled eyes.

He was shaken to the core by that look, by her words. "Tell me."

She swallowed hard. "I had an ectopic pregnancy when I was married to Eric," she began, and something turned inside Alex at the thought of Olivia pregnant to another man. Something fierce and primal rose in his throat. Something he firmly pushed aside.

"My tubes were damaged…irreparably." She took a deep breath. "So it's not that I won't have your child, Alex. It's that I can't."

He heard every word she said, but he still had to ask, "You're sure there's nothing to be done?"

She frowned. "The doctor did say it was highly unlikely rather than never." She gave a dismissive shake of her head. "But he was just being kind. He meant never. I know he did."

Alex's heart started to race. "Was he a specialist?"

"No."

"So there's still some chance?"

She swallowed. "Not really. I was told at the hospital that the damage was too extensive. I have no need to question that."

He wasn't so sure. Doctors weren't infallible. Hospitals made mistakes. But he'd let that be for now.

"Does your mother know all this?"

Her eyes softened. "Yes, and she was a great help when I needed her. She surprised me."

"I'm glad." His estimation of Felicia rose. Thank God Olivia had had someone to help her through it all.

Her lips gave a wry twist. "Unfortunately, Mum thinks it's like in the movies and that it's all going to magically right itself."

His brow furrowed. "Does she give you a hard time about it?"

"Not at all. We usually don't mention it. But I know she still hopes to be a grandmother one day." Her eyes moistened and she blinked rapidly. "I wish I could give her that grandchild but I can't."

Emotion swelled inside him and he wanted to pull Olivia into his arms and comfort her, but suddenly he needed to get out or risk being the one who needed comfort. His chest felt tight with a strange anguish.

He quickly got up from the table. "Thank you for telling me, Olivia. I have to go out now." He needed thinking time.

Alone.

"Yes," she said, as if she understood.

He strode to the door and quietly left the suite, not knowing where he was going until he walked into the bar downstairs. He wanted to get blind drunk and forget the pain rioting through him.

Dammit, he wasn't used to feeling so much, so deeply. Usually he managed to keep everything under control but that was difficult when it was in his face like this. He didn't like feeling so vulnerable where Olivia was concerned, so weak and so bloody powerless.

And he wasn't just thinking about himself either. He was thinking of Olivia. And, hell, he hadn't even begun to think about the problem of an heir and his inheritance.

Okay, so he'd decided from the start that he wasn't letting his father force him into producing a child. Yet all at once he felt guilty on his brothers' behalf. And that was crazy. Why feel bad when he'd had no intention of fulfilling the second part of the ultimatum anyway? His brothers hadn't known about any of it, but they wouldn't have expected him to sacrifice himself for them on the marriage altar, let alone add a baby to the mix.

Bloody hell. This was worse than worse.

A couple of hours later, Alex returned to their hotel room, not drunk but wishing he was. It would be such a welcome state to be in right now.

All was quiet as he slipped quietly into the darkened bedroom and started to strip off his clothes. He could see Olivia's shape beneath the blankets and didn't want to wake her. Perhaps the jetlag had caught up with her. He wanted her to get as much sleep as she could.

"You don't have to sleep with me, Alex," she said in the hushed stillness. "I'll understand if you want to go to the other room."

He swore softly and slid into bed naked. "I'm your husband. I intend to sleep beside my wife."

"Temporary wife," she pointed out, but he could hear an odd catch of pleasure in her throat.

He pulled her up close against him and let his lips brush her temple. "I'll arrange for you to see a specialist. We need a second opinion."

"But, Alex, what's the use?"

His arms tightened around her. "We need to do this. Just to be sure, okay?"

"I guess so."

"Now shh," he murmured, then kissed her cheek before hovering over her mouth. He wanted to ease her pain and the only way he knew how was for them to find release in each other.

He began to make long, slow love to her. She was soft and warm, and her welcoming body certainly made him forget everything but the moment.

But when he reached for a condom, she put her hand out and stopped him. "No need for that, Alex," she murmured. "Not anymore."

He swallowed hard. "No?"

She shook her head and a lump rose in his throat. She was showing him that even though they might see a specialist for a second opinion, she would have been willing to have his child if it had been at all possible.

He brought her to orgasm, letting himself fall into the same climax with her, joining with her. It was the most incredible experience. And the most moving.

Olivia was glad when a couple of public relations staff members joined them on their private jet to New York the next day. It gave her the chance to avoid any further intimate conversations with Alex.

Heaven knows, they'd been intimate enough last night. It had been wonderful to feel Alex inside her without the use of a condom. Up until now she hadn't been able to suggest he not use one or he'd have had to ask why.

Now he knew.

But today there was just something in his eyes that made her anxious. She didn't want him getting his hopes up about having a baby. It had taken her quite a while to come to terms with it herself. The last thing she wanted was to see him going through the same thing.

He probably just wanted to make sure for his father's sake. Oh, she knew Alex would see the game through now that he had made a commitment to her. He wouldn't go back on his word, not until the year was over anyway. But once her time was up, he'd have to ditch her and find another wife. It was the

way it had to be, she told herself, her chest tightening at the thought of him with another woman.

Of another woman having his baby.

Oh God. Somehow she had to refuse to get upset
over that. This had been a business deal and it wasn't
as if she had really meant anything to him, despite
them sharing these weeks together. It was just the
way it was. Yes, it was personal but it wasn't as
though they were in love with each other and needed
a baby to seal their love.

No, they were lovers.

And sometimes friends, that's all.

The plane landed and the next week went bles-
sedly fast in such a whirlwind of functions and ap-
pearances that neither of them had time to think.

The launch of Valente's Woman was a huge
success. In some stores the crowds were lined up out
the doors to be able to buy their bottle of the expensive perfume. It helped that her mother—bless her—
had asked her celebrity friends to drop in at some of
the stores and that in turn created a buzz that set the
customers clamoring for more.

Everyone was pleased.

Of the specialist appointment, Alex said nothing.

On their last day in New York, one of her ex-stepfathers suddenly appeared at a cocktail party.

"Olivia, darling," Randall Markham said, coming up to give her a kiss on the cheek.

Olivia looked at the man in stunned surprise. Randall had been her favorite of her two stepfathers. And he was the only one who'd remained good friends with her mother.

"Randall! What are you doing here?" she said, giving him a hug.

"Spying on you, of course, darling," he joked, keeping an old joke between them alive.

Olivia smiled genuinely for the first time in days. "You'll never convince me that my mother didn't pay you to come to my first fashion show." Olivia had been so nervous she'd banned her mother from attending. But Randall had come. Nothing had dissuaded him.

"She didn't, I swear," Randall teased, then his eyes slid to Alex beside her in a considering manner. "And this is your next husband, I presume?"

Olivia was aware of the tightening of Alex's mouth. He obviously didn't like being thought of as a "next" husband.

But she nodded and pasted a happily married smile on her face. "Yes, this is Alex." She introduced the two men. "Alex, this is Randall. One of my stepfathers."

"Ex-stepfathers," Randall pointed out, shaking Alex's hand. "I was the rich, handsome one."

Alex appeared to relax. "Obviously."

Randall turned to look at Olivia. "Unfortunately, I'm not rich anymore." He sighed. "As much as I still love your mother," he said in an exaggerated fashion, "she absolutely took me to the cleaners."

Olivia suddenly felt uneasy. She didn't want Randall saying too much in front of Alex.

"Thank heavens she didn't ruin my looks," he said in a manner that seemed ludicrous because he wasn't joking. "And thank heavens she has you to pay off her debts now," he said, sending dismay through Olivia. "I've told her to get another husband but she won't."

Olivia felt Alex stiffen beside her. "Randall, how is Cybil?" she said to change the subject.

"Fine, darling. She's doing a show on Broadway. That's why we're here in New York. That and to see our first granddaughter."

Olivia knew that Randall had no idea of the pain his words caused her. She had lost her baby after he'd divorced her mother and Felicia hadn't shared that news with him. Her mother had never believed she wouldn't have a child so she probably didn't think of it as an issue.

She forced a smile. "Shari has a baby? How old is she?" It nearly killed her to ask.

"Just a couple of months and she's a little darling,"

Randall said, then went on to sing the praises of his first grandchild.

Olivia could see the glint of anger at the back of Alex's eyes. Oh, why had Randall said anything about her mother's debts? She didn't need this right now.

After that, they spoke of other things, then they kissed goodbye and promised to meet up another time. All the while Olivia could feel Alex's anger seeping through, despite his outwardly calm manner.

He said nothing until the function had finished and they were back in their hotel suite. Then, "Something else you didn't bother to tell me?" he said, an edge to his voice.

She played for time as she placed her purse down. "What do you mean?"

Irritation flared in his eyes. "The money I gave you to marry me paid for your mother's debts, didn't it?"

She inclined her head. "*Some* of the money did, yes. The rest helped pay off my own business debts." She frowned, pretending ignorance. "You have an issue with that?"

His gaze sliced over her. "I have an issue with you not telling me things."

Her chin lifted as her heart sank. "You mean about my infertility, right?"

For a moment his face closed up. "Yes," he

muttered. Then his mouth tightened. "And now this. I feel I don't know you at all."

"You *don't* know me, Alex. If you did, you'd know that there are some things I like to keep private, just as there are some things *you* like to keep private." She paused deliberately. "Such as the fact that your father expects you to father a child."

A momentary look of discomfort crossed his face, then he gave a jerky nod. "Point taken."

"Good."

"Just tell me one thing," he fired back at her. "Are there any other surprises I should know about?"

"No." She started to walk away. She'd had enough. They were tired and their nerves were stretched and this wasn't a good time to discuss anything further.

He blew out a breath. "It comes down to trust again, doesn't it?" he said, stopping her in her tracks. "You married me, but you didn't trust me about your mother's money problems. You thought I might let it leak to the media and make some publicity out of it."

It was all true.

Every word.

She sighed. "The point is that I married you, Alex. You must've had some sort of redeeming quality about you, though for the life of me right now I can't see what it is. I'm entitled to my privacy."

His eyes shuttered then he turned and poured himself a drink. "Go to bed, Olivia. I'll come in later."

Sometime during the night, Olivia was aware of Alex coming to bed. She'd been half-asleep, but now she held her breath, waiting for him to pull her close.

Only he didn't.

"I'm sorry," he said, his voice low and rough.

Silence fell in the darkness. This was the last thing she expected him to say. "Thank you."

And then he rolled onto his side, his back to her, and promptly went to sleep.

Olivia lay there for ages, listening to his breathing, a sense of hopelessness filling her. They were destined to be childless and that meant they were destined to be divorced. It was just a matter of time.

Alex had gone when she woke up and only the crumpled blankets on the other side of the bed told her he'd been there. Heavy-hearted, she drew on her silk bathrobe and walked out into the living room, fully expecting it to be empty.

But Alex was just placing the telephone back in its cradle. He glanced up when he heard her. "That was the specialist. He said he can see you later this morning."

She missed a step. "Wh-what? So soon?"

His jaw tensed. "We need to have it confirmed once and for all."

She quickly gathered her thoughts together. "*You* need to, Alex. I don't need to know at all."

His gaze softened as he came toward her. "Olivia, don't you want to know? Really?"

Panic stirred in her chest. "No."

He stopped in front of her and placed his hands on her shoulders. "You're scared. I understand, but isn't it best to know?"

Easy for him to say, she thought cynically. He'd drop her once he knew for sure and go make a new life for himself. While she…

She shrugged. "Maybe I'll just wait and see what happens in a few years. Who knows? I might marry again and find myself pregnant and that will be a bonus," she said, letting him know he wasn't the only one capable of getting on with his life.

He pressed his lips together and gave her a little shake. "The only person you're going to get pregnant to will be me, Olivia."

His words warmed her but she knew it wasn't fair to let him get his hopes up. "Alex, look—"

He sighed and dropped his hands away. "Olivia, I won't force you into this. The choice is yours."

She stared at him and all at once realized he really needed to know. She wanted to believe it was about them as a couple, but she knew it was about the baby.

Okay, so for *him* she would do it. Otherwise he would always wonder. And perhaps after this he would be able to move on.

From her.

"Okay, Alex," she said quietly. "I'll do it."

His brows drew together. "Are you sure?"

"Yes," she said with mild exasperation.

He fixed her with a candid gaze. "Right. Go get dressed. I need to make a few phone calls then I'll be ready to come with you. We have an hour."

Her mouth dropped open. "You're coming with me?"

He looked surprised by the question. "Of course. Just try and stop me."

Oh heavens. If she wasn't careful she was going to get all weepy.

She cleared her throat. "Thank you, Alex. It's just that Eric…" How did she say this politely? "He never…bothered."

"The bastard," Alex spat, his expression clouding in anger. After a second or two, his anger seemed to cool a little. "Well, I'm different. We're in this together, Olivia."

Her throat felt so tight with emotion, she could only nod.

"Now go get dressed," Alex said, turning away and reaching for the phone, but his voice sounded a little unsteady.

Olivia fled the room before she broke down altogether. It was easier being strong when she didn't think too hard about things, but have someone give her sympathy and she would probably turn into an emotional wreck.

Once they arrived at the hospital the specialist spoke to both her and Alex, then she was given a private room and a thorough round of tests began.

The doctor was totally noncommittal during their discussion and Olivia told herself not to get her hopes up. For the main part she didn't, but there was that rogue flicker of optimism that wouldn't be quiet no matter how much she tried to suppress it.

As for Alex, he was great. He stayed with her as much as he could, refusing to leave her side.

And then late that day they waited in the room for the news together.

And Alex sat next to the bed and held her hand tightly as the specialist delivered the bad news that she would never have a child. The damage from the ectopic pregnancy was just too extensive, he was sorry to say.

Not as sorry as she was, she thought, glad to be feeling hugely numb both inside and out.

She'd known.

Dear God, she'd known, but somehow she'd let herself hope.

Now there truly was no hope left.

Nine

"We should get another opinion," Alex said once he'd recovered his breath. It was almost impossible to grasp what the specialist was saying. Hell, he didn't *want* to grasp it.

From where he stood at the end of the bed, the doctor looked down at them with sympathetic eyes. "Mr. Valente, I understand, but it won't make any difference to the outcome. Our tests were very thorough." He paused. "I'm sorry."

But Alex wasn't convinced. He glanced at Olivia. "We should try elsewhere. We could—"

"No, Alex," she said firmly. "Enough is enough."

Up until this moment "no" just hadn't been in his mindset. Now, dear God, he just couldn't believe he was being told there was no other answer.

Then he looked at this beautiful woman who was sitting up in the hospital bed, dressed in a white hospital gown, and who had just been through a medical procedure, and her head was held high with courage and determination to get on with her life. He swallowed hard. If she could take the news and put it behind her then how fair was it for him to keep pushing her over this?

"You're right," he said, and lifted her hand held tight in his own to kiss her knuckles, letting her see the admiration in his eyes.

She held his gaze for a few seconds and soft pink colored her cheeks before she looked up at the specialist. "Thank you for all your help, doctor."

The doctor nodded. "I wish it could have been better news, Mrs. Valente."

"I know."

Alex stood up and shook the doctor's hand, then the other man left them alone.

Silence.

He looked at Olivia. "Are you okay?"

It took a moment, but a small, reassuring smile appeared. "Yes, Alex. I'm fine."

He wasn't. He still felt gutted. And how she managed to smile through all this was a—

He saw her bury her face in her hands and her shoulders began to shake. "Olivia?"

She gave a small sob.

He sat on the edge of the bed and gently pulled her up against his chest, his heart cramping with pain when he saw the hot tears slipping down her cheeks. "Oh, sweetheart, let it out," he muttered. "Let it all out."

That only made it worse. He held her like that for long moments while she cried.

Eventually she pulled back, sniffing and trying to unscrunch a tissue she'd been holding in her hand. "I'm sorry."

He let his hands slide to her shoulders, needing to keep on holding her. "No, I'm the one who's sorry. I shouldn't have put you through that."

She dabbed her eyes with the tissue. "It's better that I know for sure."

He swore. "Better for whom? You…or me?" His chest ached with an inner pain. "I was wrong in asking that of you, sweetheart."

She shuddered. "Alex, don't punish yourself. I did this for both of us."

A feeling in his heart began to morph into something he'd never felt before. It terrified him, so he quickly pushed it aside, not wanting to know. "Thank you," he said in a hoarse whisper.

She drew a shaky breath. "I think I'll go to sleep now. It's getting late. Do you mind?"

He cleared his throat. "Not at all."

The specialist had said he would keep her in the hospital overnight and Alex was more than glad of that now. She needed to rest.

And he suddenly needed to be alone.

"Get them to call me if you want anything and I'll come straight over."

She leaned forward and kissed him softly on the lips. "Thanks."

He hopped off the edge of the bed and helped her to make herself comfortable, then he kissed her and left the room, the door shushing closed behind her.

It wasn't until he walked into his hotel room that he dropped down onto the sofa, his legs no longer able to hold him up. He'd gotten this far but now the reality of it was sinking in.

Olivia would never have a baby.

His baby.

Dammit, he'd realized he wanted that more than anything in the world. And it wasn't just because his father wanted him to have a child.

Then something lodged in his throat and he realized he was wrong about this. Totally wrong. The only thing he wanted more than anything in the world was Olivia herself.

He loved her.

A sense of joy swept over him that went clear through to his soul. He had a heartbeat to savor it, contemplate it. Half a second later, pain slammed into him with the force of a wrecking ball.

He couldn't tell her, especially not right now. She had enough to cope with without him putting unnecessary pressure on her. And telling a woman he loved her and wanted her to stay married to him forever was definitely immense pressure. He couldn't do that to her right now.

If at all.

Olivia was glad to leave New York later that week and head back to LA, where they were to spend a couple of days with her mother. Felicia was full of talk about whether she could juggle both the television series and the movie next year, assuming she got the part. It was good to see her mother so enthusiastic and full of promise for the future.

If only she felt as hopeful for the future, too.

But she couldn't be.

She didn't want to burst her mother's bubble so she kept quiet about the conclusive tests for her infertility. Her mother would be devastated.

As she knew Alex was, too. It was the reason he'd been slightly aloof since she'd come out of hospital and hadn't tried to make love to her. Oh, he'd been wonderful—looking after her and giving her attention, but they were normal everyday things most husbands gave their wives.

Yet she understood where Alex was coming from. He had responsibilities to his father and to his brothers and nothing could change that. He had to step back from her.

Yes, she understood.

But it hurt.

She needed him to tell her everything would be all right.

She needed him to say he wasn't going to dump her before the twelve months was up.

And right now, as silly as it seemed, she needed him to *need* her.

"Randall told me he saw you in New York," Felicia said their first evening at dinner after they'd caught up on other things.

Olivia was glad Alex would be late this evening. It was best they didn't discuss anything like this in front of him. She didn't want to give him any reminders about what had happened.

"Yes, and he's a granddad now, I hear," she said,

pasting on a bright smile to show she could handle it all. She had to put one foot in front of the other and keep moving forward, not stop to think about what she had lost.

Felicia's mouth curved with affection. "Yes, he told me." Then her smile faded. "I hope it didn't upset you, darling?"

Olivia pretended to be surprised. "No, of course not. I love Randall and I'm happy for him." That was the truth.

"That's my girl," Felicia said, leaning over and briefly squeezing Olivia's hand. "I'm glad you're over it." Just as quickly her mother leaned back in the high-backed dining chair. "Darling, I've been wanting to tell you for some time that Eric has a child, too, but I wasn't sure—"

"Shut the hell up, Felicia," Alex growled from the doorway, taking them by surprise, and both women spun around in their seats.

Felicia started to gulp like a fish. "Well, I never!"

Alex glared at her. "Can't you see your daughter is upset? Or is that just a bit beyond your comprehension?"

"Alex, don't..." Olivia warned.

He waved a dismissive hand. "No, Olivia. I won't be quiet over this. Tell her the truth. Then she might look beyond herself and see your pain like I do."

Olivia blinked in shock. There was nothing aloof about him now. Her heart skipped a beat.

"What truth, Olivia?" Felicia demanded. "What is Alex talking about?"

Olivia slowly turned. This was going to be painful for her mother. She swallowed, her throat aching. "I can't have a child, Mum. It's been confirmed."

Felicia paled. "Never?"

"No, Mum."

Her mother's mouth worked without speaking for a moment. "Oh God, I'll never be a grandmother?"

"No, Mum," Olivia said as gently as she could. "I'm afraid this isn't like the movies. There won't be a happy ending."

Seconds ticked by as Felicia stared aghast at her daughter. Then amazingly, something seemed to change inside her mother. Olivia could feel it in the air.

When she looked across at Alex, he had left the room.

"Darling," Felicia's apologetic tone began. "Your husband is right. I've only been concerned about me, not you. I'm so sorry."

Shock ran through Olivia. "Mum, it's okay."

Her mother shook her head. "No, it's not. I know my faults. I'm self-centered and irresponsible at times but…" She took a shaky breath and her eyes filled with tears. "Darling, I love you more than life itself. You know that, don't you?"

The tears welled in Olivia's eyes, too. "Yes, Mum, I know that. I've always known that. And when it comes right down to it, that's all that matters."

"Thank you for that, darling," Felicia said, and grabbed her napkin, dabbing it at her eyes in a theatrical pose that Olivia knew wasn't a pose at all this time.

Her mother gave a watery smile. "You might need to go see how your husband is," she prodded. "And please tell him I'm sorry." She winced. "No, I'll tell him myself when I see him tomorrow. I need to take responsibility."

Olivia blinked away the last of her tears and looked again at her mother with new eyes. It had been a long time coming, but Felicia really had changed. Olivia got to her feet and hugged her mother.

Felicia hugged her back, then as Olivia moved away, she asked in concern, "Are you okay with what I said about Eric having a child?"

Olivia nodded. "Absolutely." And she was. Eric didn't affect her any longer. At last she was able to leave all that behind her.

Her mother looked pleased. She waved a hand toward the door. "Go see Alex."

Olivia found Alex in the bedroom, undoing his shirt. Just the sight of him made her heart beat fast.

"That wasn't a very nice thing to say to my mother," she said, matter-of-factly.

A pulse beat in his cheek. "She needed to hear it."

"I know. Thank you," she said sincerely, seeing him look startled. "It did the trick. I think she's finally growing up."

He stopped undressing and his eyes searched hers. "It's about time she did."

Olivia wrinkled her nose. "It's been hard for her to change."

"It's hard for anyone to change."

"Yes, but perhaps it was more difficult for her. She grew up being a spoiled little girl because of her looks, then she became a beautiful spoiled woman, and then a spoiled movie star. Everyone treats her like royalty."

He stared for a moment before shaking his head with slight amazement. "You don't realize it, do you?"

She blinked. "What?"

"Your mother may be royalty in the movie world but out here in the real world, *you're* the one who is true royalty. You not only have elegance and class, but you have a sense of compassion and understanding and generosity that shines through."

Her breath hitched, his opinion of her making her feel like jelly inside. No man had ever said such a nice thing to her. "You can't know that," she murmured.

He came toward her and put his hand under her chin, looking deeply into her eyes. "I *know* the person you are, Olivia Valente."

Then he lowered his head and kissed her, her pulse racing even more when his hands slid down to pull her up against him. He was fully aroused.

She kissed him back. He needed her and that was enough.

For now.

They returned to their apartment in Sydney overlooking the harbor and Olivia was immediately swept up in business dealings with her boutiques. It was a relief to keep busy.

Of their future together Alex didn't say a word, nor did he mention anything about telling his father and she was coward enough to accept that. Suddenly every moment spent with him was important.

Why, she didn't want to know.

And then she came home one evening and heard the muffled sound of voices coming from the study. She tapped lightly on the door and opened it and found Alex and his two brothers sitting on the couch, glasses of whiskey in their hands.

Their expressions were welcoming but she suspected they'd been discussing something important and didn't really appreciate the interruption.

"Oh, I'm sorry. I didn't know you were all here," she said, ready to step back and leave them to it.

But Alex was already coming toward her. "Sweetheart, you don't have to apologize," he said, the loving husband. "We're just discussing business." He swooped in for a kiss in a possessive manner she knew was only for show.

She kissed him back, welcoming the feel of his lips on hers after a day spent away from him.

"Um...I'd better go get some dinner," she said, once he eased back and let her go.

"There's a casserole in the oven."

Up close, Olivia could see his eyes already turning back toward business. "Great." She forced a smile. "Have you eaten?"

"Yes." She looked at the other two men to ask them if they'd like something, but Alex spoke before her. "They've eaten, too."

"Oh."

"Yes," Nick said with a polite smile. "We've eaten."

"But thanks anyway," Matt, the youngest, said.

She could see they were wanting to get back to their discussion. "I'll leave you to it."

She stepped back and closed the door, then went to take a shower before eating, but she grew more worried with each passing moment. Had Alex told them about his father's ultimatum after all? And not just about needing to marry but about having a child as well? He had nothing to hide from them any longer. He had already married her. And now there would be no baby.

Her heart ached. Then something occurred to her. Perhaps Alex had asked them here to discuss a new plan?

Or a new wife?

She gulped. No, she couldn't believe he would say anything about her infertility to his brothers. Not without her consent.

Still, later when he slid into bed in the dark she had to ask. "Is everything okay?"

"Yes."

"You all looked quite preoccupied."

"There's a small problem. We can deal with it."

She swallowed hard, hoping *she* wasn't the problem they would deal with. Then she pushed it out of her mind and tried to get some sleep.

But the next morning as she came out of the bathroom after finishing her shower, she heard Alex talking on the phone and she stopped dead.

"Dad, I need to see you about something," he was saying quietly, his back to her. "I'll be there in half an hour."

There was a pause.

"Cancel your appointment, Dad. This is important. It can't wait."

Another pause.

"Right. See you soon." He hung up, pushed himself to his feet and reached for his trousers. Then he saw her and he seemed to freeze. Or was that just her imagination?

He scowled. "You look pale. Are you okay?"

She forced herself to move. "Yes, I'm fine. The shower was a bit too hot, that's all." She half expected he would tease her about them making steam in the shower, only he didn't. He had that distant look back on his face.

"You take it easy, Olivia. You've been rushing around too much lately."

"Thank you for your concern," she said, unable to stop a hint of coolness to her voice.

He held her eyes for a beat, looking slightly puzzled, then turned away to glance at the bedside clock. "I have to go." He headed for the door, stopping briefly to kiss her on the mouth. "See you tonight."

He left the room.

But he left behind a very worrying silence.

Ten

Alex didn't come home until after ten that night. He had phoned earlier to say there was a problem and he had to work late, but Olivia had heard voices laughing in the background and wondered if that were true. She wanted to believe him and for the most part she did, but memories of her ex-husband's cheating kept flashing through her mind.

She knew Alex wasn't like that. Alex had integrity and was honest and—

Was this the same Alex she now suspected might not even wait the twelve months before getting rid of her? The same Alex who might be plotting even now with his father and his brothers to find a way to end his marriage?

The same man who—

No, she was jumping to conclusions. She seriously didn't want to believe any of that. Perhaps those voices had merely been his staff. There certainly hadn't been any music in the background to indicate a bar, nor any woman's voice specifically.

Still, when he stripped in the dark in the bedroom then went to take a shower, she found herself quietly sniffing the air for the scent of perfume. Thank God there was none. And when he joined her in bed ten minutes later, there was only the smell of Alex.

And it was wonderful.

And when he slid his arm around her and pulled her up against him, she waited for him to kiss her and make love to her. Only, he kissed the top of her head instead then promptly fell asleep.

Strangely, Olivia felt comforted and she must have fallen asleep, too, because the next thing she knew the telephone beside the bed was ringing. Her heart jumped in her throat and instinctively she reached for the phone in the pre-dawn light.

Her heart thudded with relief when she heard

her mother's voice. Felicia always got the time zones mixed up. "Mum, it's five in the morning over here."

"Darling, I had to call you," Felicia said urgently. "I'm afraid the newspapers know."

"Know?" Olivia's forehead crinkled as she sat up in bed. "What do they know?" She still wasn't functioning right.

"About you not being able to have a…a…baby."

Olivia's brain stumbled. "Wh-what?"

"It's in all the newspapers over here today. And my phone hasn't stopped ringing." Felicia took a shuddering breath. "I'm so sorry, darling."

"I don't believe this," Olivia whispered, vaguely aware of Alex switching the light on and coming around to her side of the bed.

"I don't know how they knew," her mother continued. "*I* certainly didn't tell them. I hope you believe that."

She was having trouble coming to grips with this. Why would anyone want to know about her and her infertility problems?

"Olivia?" Alex demanded, then when she didn't answer he took the phone out of her hand. "Felicia, what on earth did you say to Olivia?" He listened, then his eyes shot to Olivia and his jaw clenched.

"How the devil did that happen?" he growled. Felicia must have spoken as he paused, then said, "Yes, I'll look after her."

Olivia was only partly aware of him hanging up the phone.

"Olivia?"

She looked at him then. "How could they, Alex?" she choked.

His eyes darkened. "I know, sweetheart."

She bit back a sob. "I don't want the world to know about…about… It's private."

He pulled her into his arms. "Shh."

She went willingly, leaning on him for a moment, accepting his strength, before giving a shuddering sob. She wanted to cry but wouldn't give them—*any* of them—the satisfaction.

And then something hit her.

It was so obvious.

She pulled back, the words bursting from her, her nerves stretched to the limit. "I bet it was your father. He wants to get rid of me. He wants you to marry someone who can give you a child."

His eyes narrowed. "Do you hear yourself?"

It suddenly seemed more than plausible. "You told him, didn't you? You told him and now he knows and—"

"Don't be bloody ridiculous. I didn't tell him a thing."

"Then it was one of your brothers. That's why they were here the other night. You were telling them the whole thing, weren't you?"

He shook her lightly. "Stop it! No one knew but you, me and your mother."

She gasped, his shake hurtling her back to their surroundings. "Oh God, I'm sorry, Alex. I don't know what came over me." Heavens, she'd gone crazy for a minute there.

"It's understandable," he said, but there was a stiffness to his shoulders that hadn't been there before. He got to his feet and stood looking down at her, keeping a distance now that she very much regretted.

She hesitated, measuring how to explain it all. "I wonder how the media found out about it? Someone had to have told them. My mother's just as confused as we are."

His brow rose. "Maybe someone from the doctor's office in New York?"

"Yes, that's possible."

His eyes hardened. "Or your ex?"

She sucked in a sharp breath and considered the possibility out loud. "Yes…but why now? He knew it was unlikely I'd ever have a child. He could have told them about it years ago." She shook her blond head. "No, he'd come out of it smelling less than roses. Eric wouldn't want that," she added cynically.

"No, I don't suppose the bastard would."

She was surprised by the comment yet not. The thought of Eric always set her on edge, too.

She mentally pushed Eric aside. "I just don't understand why the papers need to print stuff like this. Why do they need to cause people pain? Isn't it enough that we have to live it?" she whispered, then gave a ragged sigh. "I guess I should be used to it."

He made a harsh sound. "Whoever leaked that bit of information had better watch out. I'll hunt them down. They won't do it again in a hurry."

He looked so angry she was reminded of how fiercely this man protected his own.

"Alex, I know I got it all wrong about your father and brothers, but what were you and Nick and Matt speaking about the other night? You went to see your father yesterday morning, too. I heard you on the telephone telling him there was a problem."

His angry expression faded and concern replaced it. "Dad's not well. We were discussing how to push him gently into retirement."

Her shoulders slumped. "Oh boy, I really got it wrong, didn't I?"

He held her gaze for a minute, seeming to delve into her thoughts, but then he broke eye contact and glanced at the clock. "Speaking of my father, I'm going down to the study to call him. He needs to know. If we don't tell him, the media will. No doubt they'll be hanging around the office today."

Dismay filled her. "That'll mean they'll be at the boutique, too."

"Yes. Perhaps you should stay home today and not leave the apartment."

She nodded woodenly. "Okay. And I'll phone Lianne and tell her not to go into work either."

"Don't turn on the television," he said, heading for the door. "Do some work or just try and relax. I know it's hard."

"Okay." Her throat closed up and her heart cramped. "I'm so sorry for causing all this trouble, Alex."

He stopped at the door and looked back. "Don't be crazy," he rasped, then left the room, taking her heart with him.

It was then she realized why he made her forget who she was. Why she found herself in him.

Oh God, she loved him.

Loved him more than life itself.

Oh my—she loved Alex. He had taken possession of her heart in a way she'd never thought possible.

He filled her completely, making her come truly alive for the first time ever. For a moment she took hold of that love, celebrating its beauty, honored that it had come to live in her heart.

Then reality struck with a bang.

She had no idea what Alex felt for her, but it didn't matter anyway. She couldn't let it matter. Despite knowing he was the right person for her, this just wasn't the right time or the right place. There could *never* be a right time for them. Not when she could only bring pain and heartache to him.

There was only one thing to do. She had to compose herself, somehow. She'd been given a beautiful gift that chose to rest in her heart, but showing him that gift of love would only cause more heartache.

Pain clawed at Alex's heart as he strode to the study to call his father. The pain was for the anguish Olivia was going through right now, and for the strength she'd need to get through the next few days. He'd be there for her of course, but damn the media's greed for a story—any story.

Damn them all.

He swallowed hard. Hell, she'd just apologized for causing *him* trouble. No apology was necessary for something like this.

In fact he wanted to apologize to *her* for putting her through all this. If he hadn't married her, if he hadn't tried to use her to help launch Valente's Woman, then she'd be going about her own business, designing clothes and getting on with her life.

But no, he had to come into her life and make sure the one thing she wanted kept to herself was splashed through the papers.

Bloody hell.

Entering the study, he sat in his chair and reached for the telephone. It was early and his father was going to get a rude awakening. Good. Cesare Valente shouldn't have started all this marriage business in the first place. If he'd just let things be…

Alex flinched. Then Olivia wouldn't have come into his life. He wouldn't have fallen in love with her. He wouldn't have known what true love was all about.

He sighed. As much as it was painful for him, at least his love for her was something to hang on to.

It took a few moments for his father to answer the telephone. "Dad, it's Alex."

"Alex?" Cesare's sleepy voice came down the line.

"Dad, I have to tell you something."

"Son, it's five-fifteen in the morning." There was a pause as Cesare replied to something Isabel said in the background.

"I wouldn't call if it wasn't important. You know that."

There was a grunt. "Let me just get comfortable, then you can tell me. I'm still trying to wake up." There was the sound of movement. "Right. Now what's the matter?"

Alex could feel his blood pressure begin to rise just at the thought of it all. "You're going to read it in the newspapers soon, or someone will call you and tell you anyway, but…"

"But what?"

Alex took a deep breath, his heart pounding in his chest. "Olivia and I can't give you a grandchild, Dad. She's infertile." He hated saying the word. Hated having to tell anyone what was essentially his and Olivia's private business. "And now, dammit, some-how the media have found out and it's in all the papers in the States."

There was nothing but the heaviest silence on the other end of the phone.

"So you're telling me Olivia can't have a child?" Cesare finally said, followed by Isabel's gasp.

"Yes."

It was hard to tell what his father was thinking and Alex could have kicked himself now for not going straight to his parents' estate, rather than saying this over the phone. At least then he'd be able to try to read his father's expression. He grimaced. And why the hell did he care what his father thought anyway?

"I'm sorry to hear that, son."

"Yeah, so am I." And that was the understatement of the century.

Time ticked by as though it was dragging its feet.

"You love her, don't you?" Cesare said with what Alex thought was deceptive calm. His father was always the ultimate businessman and rarely gave anything away of his thoughts. On another level Alex was surprised by the other man's perception.

"Yes, Dad, I do."

Cesare made some sort of sound, but Isabel said something in the background over the top of it, and it was hard to tell what reaction his father had given.

Then, "What are you going to do, Alex?"

Alex's hand tightened around the telephone. "The one thing I *won't* be doing is giving her up," he said in a warning voice.

"That sounds like an ultimatum to me."

"You should know. You're an expert at them."

There was a heavy pause. "What do you want me to say, Alex?"

"Nothing, Dad. There's nothing you can say that will change a damn thing." Alex gave a short pause.

"The only reason I'm telling you this is because we need to look at what the media will do next. They're bound to be calling you for comment or coming to the office."

"*Maledizione,*" his father cursed. "I've got better things to do than let them waste my time."

"I agree, but we have to think about Olivia," he reminded his father. "I don't want anyone talking to them about her. She's going through enough as it is."

"Look, come and see me. We need to talk."

Alex's throat tightened with emotion. "I will, but don't think I'll be changing my mind."

"Don't jump the gun, *figlio mio.*"

Alex ignored his father's further lapse into Italian. He'd go but he already knew talking would be a waste of time. And right now he really didn't give a damn what Cesare Valente had to say.

Half an hour later Olivia had showered and dressed and, with a heavy heart, she went down to the study. Alex was sitting at the desk going through some paperwork. He looked up when she entered the room.

Her heart constricted. Dear God, she was breaking up inside, but she had to go through with this. She had to set him free so that he could make a life for himself with someone else, someone who didn't cause havoc in his life, no matter how inadvertently.

"Did you tell your father?" she asked, watching his face, trying to see how it had gone.

"Yes." His expression gave nothing away. "About half an hour ago."

"What did he say?"

"Not much. He was still trying to wake up."

She could imagine that Cesare Valente wouldn't be pleased. He'd seemed to like her but now that she was stopping him—no, stopping his son—from carrying on the Valente name, things would change. It wouldn't matter that Nick and Matt would undoubtedly have children of their own. Cesare was old-school and he would want his eldest son to have the first grandchild.

"I have an important meeting this morning, but my mother said she'll call you later. She doesn't want you to be alone. She wants to come over and spend some time with you."

"There's no need." She didn't plan on being here anyway.

"Yes, there is."

"Alex, I'm okay. I don't need Isabel to come over and stay with me." She swallowed past her dry throat, steeling herself to tell him why. "Alex, I—"

The telephone rang, cutting her off.

He sat there, his stare drilling into her, as if he suspected she was about to say something important.

It rang again and she nodded her head at it. "You'd better answer that."

His eyes narrowed. "It can wait."

She'd lost her momentum now. How could she say what she had to say with a ringing telephone in the background?

"Alex, we can talk later. You should answer the phone."

Frustration crossing his face, he grabbed the receiver and barked into it. Olivia dropped down on the couch, needing something to sit on while she gathered her strength again. As soon as he hung up she would have to speak up. There was no getting around it. Alex deserved better than—

All at once she noticed he'd turned pale with what looked like shock. Oh heavens, not more of this media crap? Didn't they ever—

"I'll be right there," he muttered, then put the phone back in its cradle.

She pushed herself to her feet. "What's the matter?"

He didn't answer, just sat staring at the phone.

"Alex?"

He blinked, seeming to come from a long way off. "Um...it's my father. They think he's had a heart attack. The housekeeper just called to say my mother's gone with Dad in the ambulance."

Olivia gasped. "Oh my God!"

He stood up and started toward the door, pale but focused now. "I have to go."

She put her hand on his forearm as he passed, stopping him. "Alex, I'll come with you."

His brows drew together. "No, you stay here. There'll be enough reporters at the hospital as it is." And then he kissed her cheek and continued out of the room.

Olivia let him go, shaken by his comment. He hadn't meant to be hurtful but it had cut her to the quick, showing her exactly how unsuitable and disruptive she was for him.

For his family.

She swallowed as a new anguish seared her. And now his father was having a heart attack and she was more than likely to blame for bringing it on. Oh Lord. She prayed Cesare would be okay. If he wasn't…

No, she wouldn't think about that.

She'd keep busy until she heard from Alex. He'd call as soon as he knew something, surely. For now, she'd go phone Lianne and explain it all. She was close to her business partner, but this wasn't something she looked forward to doing. She didn't want anyone's sympathy. The only thing she wanted was Alex.

The telephone rang again and she rushed to the desk to grab it. Could this be news of Cesare so soon? Alex would only just be getting in his car.

It wasn't.

It was a reporter and she hung up without answering his question. *How do you feel about your infertility?* She gave a choked sob. How the heck did he think she felt?

On top of the world!

Gloriously happy!

Ecstatic!

The phone rang again.

She froze. It could be Alex. Or Isabel. Or perhaps Felicia. With a shaky hand, she picked it up then dropped it back down just as quickly when she heard the same reporter's voice. And then she disconnected it.

Damn them.

She'd turn her cell phone on so that Alex could at least contact her. Only, when she took it out of her purse, as soon as she turned it on it began beeping with messages. None of the numbers looked familiar and she soon realized the messages were all about the same thing. Her heart thudded. No doubt for some it was easy getting her number.

At least with a cell phone she could leave it on

silent and still check the numbers in case Alex called. But first, she called him to let him know what was happening.

He swore. "Don't answer any of them unless you see my number, okay?"

She was warmed by his response. "Okay." She hesitated. "I'm so sorry about your dad, Alex."

"So am I," he muttered, then had to hang up because he'd just arrived at the hospital.

A sense of inadequacy swept over her as she walked back into the study and sat down at the desk. She couldn't be there for Alex when he needed her. She couldn't have his child. She couldn't even give her mother a grandchild. What the heck use was she?

She shuddered. Oh God. This was crazy talk. She was feeling sorry for herself, that's all. She had to stop it.

Right. She took a deep breath and gathered herself together. She'd phone Lianne shortly, but first she'd phone her mother just to let her know she was okay.

And she was, she told herself as she picked up the telephone from the desk and reconnected it, breathing a quick sigh of relief when she got a dial tone.

Surprisingly it was her mother who answered straight away, and not the housekeeper. Olivia briefly told Felicia about Cesare and promised to keep her up to date, then she told her about having to disconnect the phone temporarily and to call her on her cell phone if necessary. Her mother understood all too well.

Then, "Darling, I know who leaked the news. It was Brita."

"Your housekeeper?"

"Yes. Just now I caught her on the telephone to a reporter. Apparently she heard us talking about it when you stayed here." Her mother's displeasure came clear across the ocean. "She's packing her bags right now."

Olivia was shocked. "But she's been with you for years." And lasted the longest.

"Five, but apparently she feels hard done by." Felicia clicked her tongue. "It's hard to get good staff these days."

Olivia could have reminded her mother that even back "in the good old days" her mother had had trouble keeping her staff. It wasn't that Felicia wasn't nice to them, but more that she was too "precious," as one of them had commented when Olivia had contacted her to beg her to come back.

"Darling, I'm so sorry about this," Felicia said. "I don't know how I can make it up to you."

"Mum, you don't have to do anything. It's not your fault, okay?"

"Okay. Don't forget to call me when you know something about Cesare."

"I won't."

But as Olivia hung up the phone, she knew her mother was feeling guilty about it all, in spite of what she'd said.

And perhaps that wasn't such a bad thing where Felicia was concerned. It showed she was still growing and changing and becoming more aware of others. Olivia was relieved not to worry so much about her mother anymore. It was one less thing for her to think about.

Alex spent the morning with his brothers pacing up and down the hospital, racked with guilt. He shouldn't have woken his father up so early. He'd known his dad wasn't in the best of health and needed his sleep.

Not only had he woken him, he'd then gone on to hand Cesare a plateful of stress. Just the idea of all the hassle the media would cause was enough to stress a person out, let alone telling his father about Olivia being infertile, and worse, that he was sticking by Olivia's side no matter what.

Not that any of this would change his mind. He still intended to stay with Olivia and love her as much as he could. But perhaps dumping all this on a man who'd come close to having a heart attack wasn't the cleverest thing he'd ever done. He could have waited a few hours and gone over and broken it to his father more carefully than he did.

Just then Isabel came through the doors of the waiting room, and he held his breath, his heart thudding inside his chest. Then he saw she was smiling.

"He's going to be just fine," she told the three brothers quickly. "It was only a mild heart attack and they have every confidence he won't have another one. That is, if he changes his lifestyle. I intend to make that happen."

Alex felt sick with relief. His father was a pain in the butt at times, but this was his father and he loved him, dammit.

Nick and Matt started firing questions at Isabel. Alex listened while she replied as best she could, but he held back, taking it all in.

"He's sleeping now, so why don't you all go to work and come back later this afternoon? It's no use just sitting here doing nothing." She kissed Nick's then Matt's cheek. "Now I want to speak to Alex for a moment so you two go on ahead," she said, shooing them out of there. "It's nothing important."

Alex stiffened, aware of the curious looks from his

brothers before they left. Was there something more Isabel wasn't telling them? Isabel said it wasn't important but—

"Alex, I want you to know how sorry I am that Olivia can't have children," she said, giving his arm a squeeze.

Alex had been so involved in everything else over the last couple of minutes, he'd forgotten his own problems.

He nodded. "Thanks."

"Your father asked me to give you a message."

He tensed, feeling the blow already. "And that is?"

"He said he's sorry. He said he only wants you to be happy, and that if you love Olivia then that's enough for him."

Alex gulped. "He said that?"

"Yes. And he told me everything." Her mouth tightened. "If I'd known what he was doing I would have put a stop to it, believe me."

His stepmother was a formidable woman when she got riled.

"Thanks, but if he hadn't given me an ultimatum, I doubt I would have married her." Or maybe he would have—though it may have taken quite a while. She'd caught his eye right from the moment he'd seen her.

"Somehow I think you would have still ended up together." She kissed his cheek. "You'd better get home to your wife. She needs you right now."

Alex nodded, then left with the promise to be back later. Now it was time for Olivia. He hated the media for what they were doing to his wife. It gutted him to see their private business in the papers, but it must go to the heart of her even more.

Olivia got up from the sofa and rushed toward him when he opened the door. "How is he?" she said, full of concern for the man who had done nothing but manipulate her life for his own purposes.

Hell, not that *he* had done any different.

"He'll be fine. It was only a mild attack."

"Thank God!" She threw her arms around him and hugged him.

Delighted to have her in his arms, he hugged her back, inhaling the scent of her, loving the feel of her body against his. He wanted this for the rest of his life. He wanted—

She dropped her hands and took a few steps away. "I spoke to my mother again. Alex, it was her housekeeper who told the reporters. Brita heard us talking about it."

His brow furrowed. "Brita? I'm surprised. I would never have thought it."

"I know."

His brow cleared. "At least we know who it was."

She nodded. "Mum fired her on the spot."

"Good." Thank God it hadn't been someone close, he wanted to say but didn't.

She must have sensed his thoughts. "Alex, again, I'm so sorry I accused your father of it."

He had to be fair. "It's not such a far-fetched conclusion," he admitted. "Who knows what he would've done if I'd told him before the papers got hold of the story?"

Or before he'd told his father he loved her.

"Let's give him the benefit of the doubt," she suggested, making him love her all the more for her generous nature.

Right then, he caught something out of the corner of his eye. Turning to look, he saw two suitcases down by the bureau. The breath seemed to leave his body. "What the hell?"

Regret filled her eyes and she straightened her shoulders. "I thought it only fair I wait to speak to you."

His heart began to sink. "Wait?"

"I'm releasing you from our agreement, Alex."

He swore. "What are you saying?"

"I'm offering you a divorce."

His head reeled back. "Who said I *want* a divorce?"

Her blue eyes shimmered with sudden tears, but she blinked them away. "I don't want you feeling responsible for me anymore. I don't want you staying with me out of pity."

"Who the hell said I'm staying with you out of pity?" he grated, his gut clenching and unclenching.

She took a shaky breath. "Accept it, Alex. This is the way it has to be."

"No." His chest tightened with emotion. How could she even think about divorce? Didn't she know he loved her?

Oh Lord. No, she didn't know that. How could she? He'd never told her of his feelings.

He opened his mouth, then as quickly shut it again. She'd never told him of her feelings either. To tell her he loved her, he had to know that her love would meet him halfway. He didn't know that with Olivia.

In fact, he *knew* she didn't love him. That was the one thing he would have sensed. A woman in love wouldn't even think about divorce…about walking away from her husband. A woman in love would sacrifice herself for…

His heart jolted.

Wasn't she sacrificing herself right now by releasing him from their agreement? Could she actually *love* him? The thought of it captivated him, just as her beauty did. If that were the case he had to tell her, had to let her know. If she were afraid of love he'd help her through it.

"I love you, Olivia."

She went perfectly still. "Wh-what?"

"I love you, darling. You can't leave me."

Olivia fumbled for words as she looked at Alex. They were words she longed to hear. Words she dare not consider. "But I can't give you a child."

His gray eyes softened. "I didn't marry you for an heir. I married you for my father's sake and for the sake of my family's company." He paused. "And then I fell in love with you. You are everything I've ever wanted, ever needed. I don't want anything more than you."

Her chest tightened with emotion. "Oh, Alex," she whispered. If only she could believe it didn't matter. But she knew it did.

"Do you love me, too, Olivia?"

She hesitated. "Family is important to you," she said, ignoring his question. "To both of us. I—"

"Do you love me, Olivia?" his words cut across hers, a muscle ticking in the side of his cheek, making her realize he wouldn't give up until he knew.

"Yes, I do, but—"

"No buts."

Oh God. She couldn't let him fool himself. "No, Alex. I would always feel like I've cheated you by not giving you a child."

"No," he ground out. "Absolutely not."

"But your father…your brothers' inheritance…"

He stepped up to her and cupped her face with his palms. "Look me in the eyes, Olivia. Look deep and see my love. It's for you, for the person you are right now, the woman I fell in love with. Unlike our marriage pact, that love is unconditional. It has nothing to do with anyone else."

"Alex, I…" She hesitated, choking up, tears springing into her eyes.

"Darling, I'm asking you to trust me totally this time. *Trust* that I love you. Trust that you are enough for me and always will be."

It was that word—trust—that tipped the balance. All this time she'd been learning to trust him, but it was only bit by bit, no matter how much she fooled herself. Now she knew deep in her heart that she did trust him, fully, utterly, believably. She trusted what he said and the man he was.

"Yes," she said, swaying toward him. "I trust you, Alex. I love you with all my heart."

His gray eyes turned to dark silver and he pulled

her close for a kiss. Her head swam as love passed between them. Love and infinite joy.

Afterward he released her just a little. "I want to kiss you until we grow old together, darling."

She caught her breath. "Oh, yes."

He grew more serious. "I didn't want to say this before because I wanted you to make the decision, but we could always adopt."

Her heart rose in her chest. "I didn't dare let myself think about that option. Your father—"

"Is happy for us," he said, startling her. "I told him how much I love you. I told him I wasn't about to leave you and that the business could go to hell for all I care. My brothers would survive without it, just as I would."

Her eyes widened. "You said all that?"

"We Valentes don't mess around when we want something."

"That's true." She looked up at him, letting him see the love in her eyes, no longer afraid of hiding it. "And seeing that I'm a Valente now…" She began undoing his tie.

"You want me?" he said huskily.

"No, I *need* you." In that heartbeat, Olivia silently agreed that when it came to love there were no conditions.

Epilogue

Six months later, they held an adoption party for their new son. Eight-year-old Scott Portman, now Scott Portman Valente, had been orphaned by a car accident two years earlier, leaving him with no relatives. Despite initially hoping to adopt a baby, Olivia and Alex had fallen in love with Scott the moment he'd said, "All I want is a mum and dad to love me again."

Talk about a serious tug on the heartstrings! They'd asked about adopting him there and then and Scott had come to live with them soon after in the new house.

Today, Scott's adoption had been made official. He was well and truly *theirs*.

And now all the family were celebrating Christmas at Villa Valente. Cesare had retired just after his heart attack but was in good health. He and Isabel looked very happy.

Alex had taken over the business with the help of his brothers, taking the House of Valente toward outstanding success through more international settings.

Even Felicia had flown in from the States in between recordings of her television show, which had proven a winner. Someone else had won the part in the movie but Olivia's mother hadn't minded by that stage. Felicia had found a new medium to showcase herself. And she was doing it well.

As for herself, a month ago she'd held a showing of the Valente Collection designs and it had been a huge success. Her boutiques were doing well and Lianne had even suggested they expand more, but Olivia was rather enjoying being a mother right now. Besides, she and Alex had spoken about going back to the orphanage in the near future to find a brother or sister for Scott.

Life was good.

"Hmm, what's that perfume you're wearing?" Alex teased, coming up behind her in the sunroom where she was placing plates of food on the table.

She spun around in his arms. "You know it's Valente's Woman."

His mouth hovered over hers. "No, *you* are Valente's woman."

She smiled, loving the possessive sound in his voice, confident they were equal partners in this marriage. "Is that so?"

His brow rose. "Are you going to argue with the man who loves you more than life itself?"

She breathed in his words of love. "Yes."

"I thought so," he murmured, lowering his head for a kiss.

And as his lips met hers, Olivia changed her mind. Life wasn't just good. It was better than good.

It was fantastic.

* * * * *

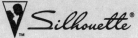

Silhouette®

Romantic SUSPENSE

Sparked by Danger, Fueled by Passion.

Cindy Dees
Killer Affair

SEDUCTION SUMMER

Seduction in the sand…and a killer on the beach.

Can-do girl Madeline Crummby is off to a remote
Fijian island to review an exclusive resort, and she hires
Tom Laruso, a burned-out bodyguard, to fly her there
in spite of an approaching hurricane. When their plane
crashes, they are trapped on an island with a serial killer
who stalks overaffectionate couples. When their false
attempts to lure out the killer turn all too real, Tom and
Madeline must risk their lives and their hearts….

**Look for the third installment
of this thrilling miniseries,
available August 2008
wherever books are sold.**

REQUEST YOUR FREE BOOKS!

2 FREE NOVELS
PLUS 2
FREE GIFTS!

Passionate, Powerful, Provocative!

YES! Please send me 2 FREE Silhouette Desire® novels and my 2 FREE gifts (gifts are worth about $10). After receiving them, if I don't wish to receive any more books, I can return the shipping statement marked "cancel". If I don't cancel, I will receive 6 brand-new novels every month and be billed just $4.05 per book in the U.S. or $4.74 per book in Canada, plus 25¢ shipping and handling per book and applicable taxes, if any*. That's a savings of almost 15% off the cover price! I understand that accepting the 2 free books and gifts places me under no obligation to buy anything. I can always return a shipment and cancel at any time. Even if I never buy another book, the two free books and gifts are mine to keep forever.   225 SDN ERVX   326 SDN ERVM

Name	(PLEASE PRINT)	
Address		Apt. #
City	State/Prov.	Zip/Postal Code

Signature (if under 18, a parent or guardian must sign)

Mail to the **Silhouette Reader Service**:
IN U.S.A.: P.O. Box 1867, Buffalo, NY 14240-1867
IN CANADA: P.O. Box 609, Fort Erie, Ontario L2A 5X3

Not valid to current subscribers of Silhouette Desire books.

Want to try two free books from another line?
Call 1-800-873-8635 or visit www.morefreebooks.com.

* Terms and prices subject to change without notice. N.Y. residents add applicable sales tax. Canadian residents will be charged applicable provincial taxes and GST. Offer not valid in Quebec. This offer is limited to one order per household. All orders subject to approval. Credit or debit balances in a customer's account(s) may be offset by any other outstanding balance owed by or to the customer. Please allow 4 to 6 weeks for delivery. Offer available while quantities last.

Your Privacy: Silhouette Books is committed to protecting your privacy. Our Privacy Policy is available online at www.eHarlequin.com or upon request from the Reader Service. From time to time we make our lists of customers available to reputable third parties who may have a product or service of interest to you. If you would prefer we not share your name and address, please check here. ☐

COMING NEXT MONTH

#1885 FRONT PAGE ENGAGEMENT—Laura Wright
Park Avenue Scandals
This media mogul needs to shed his playboy image, and who better to tame his wild ways than his sexy girl-next-door neighbor?

#1886 BILLIONAIRE'S MARRIAGE BARGAIN—
Leanne Banks
The Billionaires Club
Marry his investor's daughter and he'd have unlimited business backing. Then he discovered that his convenient fiancée was passion personified…and all bets were off.

#1887 WED TO THE TEXAN—Sara Orwig
Platinum Grooms
They were only to be married for one year, but this Texas billionaire wasn't through with his pretend wife just yet.

#1888 BABY BUSINESS—Katherine Garbera
Billionaires and Babies
Convincing his pregnant ex-fiancée to marry him will take all his negotiating skills. Falling for her for real…that will be his greatest risk.

#1889 FIVE-STAR COWBOY—Charlene Sands
Suite Secrets
He wants her in his boardroom and his bedroom, and when this millionaire cowboy realizes she's the answer to his business needs...seduction unfolds.

#1890 CLAIMING HIS RUNAWAY BRIDE—
Yvonne Lindsay
An accident leaves her without any memories of the past. Then a handsome man appears at her door claiming she's his wife.…

SDCNM0708